W9-BZD-102

Bloomington Public Library

JUL 2016

TALES OF WESTERFORD

DRAGONS, KNIGHTS AND KINGS

DARRYL WOMACK

Copyright © 2015 by Elevate Publishing

All rights reserved. No part of this publication may be reproduced, distributed, or transmitted in any form or by any means, including photocopying, recording, digital scanning, or other electronic or mechanical methods, without the prior written permission of the publisher, except in the case of brief quotations embodied in critical reviews and certain other noncommercial uses permitted by copyright law.

For permission requests, please address Elevate Publishing

Editorial Content: AnnaMarie McHargue

Cover Art: Kevin Womack

Layout: Aaron Snethen

This book may be purchased in bulk for educational, business, organizational or promotional use.

For more information, please email info@elevatepub.com.

Published by Elevate Fiction, a division of Elevate Publishing, Boise, ID

ISBN-13: 9781943425297

Ebooks ISBN: 9781943425631

Library of Congress Control Number: 2015956313

DEDICATION

To Mom and Dad for allowing me to
take chances and make mistakes.

To Greg and Liz for making me the
middle child forcing my creativity.

To Garrett, Kevin, and Chris for
helping me ignore the crocodile.

To Patty for believing in me always and
for smiling even while rolling her eyes.

ENDORSEMENTS

Darryl Womack, in Tales of Westerford: Dragons, Knights and Kings, tells a beautiful tale of friendship and loyalty that will appeal to all. I rooted for Nat from the start, and of course, his relationship with the dragon made my heart sing. You have a hero of the highest standard here, and a story that pulls the reader into long ago days of knights, dragons and chivalry. I can't wait to read the sequel!

Diane Adams,

Author of *Zoom!, I Can Do It Myself!, Teacher's Little Helper* and *Two Hands to Hold You*. She also is the illustrator of *A Home for Salty*.

Tales of Westerford is a magical story that will inspire a child's imagination and teach the noble virtues of honesty, loyalty and bravery.

Mike Mattos,

Educator and author of *Simplifying Response to Intervention*

Darryl Womack connects the magic behind the sacred tradition of oral story telling with the mesmerizing printed word – both satisfying for compatible reasons, brought together by his unique voice. You can feel the warmth of the campfire while reading, anxious for the storyteller to take us into his world, confident he will lead us to places we have never been.

Marcus Dowd,
Admission Coordinator for the Robert Day School, Claremont McKenna College, author, screenwriter

Tales of Westerford's titular world is as grand as it is familiar. Reading through Darryl Womack's "Tales" is like recalling an old and cherished dream. The story of brave Nat, a boy pursuing knighthood and love, is endearingly pure; the obstacles he faces may be great, but his heart's intentions are greater! I love the loyalty he displays toward his kingdom and sweet dragon; Nat's a knight that I would follow into any battle, no matter the stakes."

McKenna Harris,
Animator, Previous Character Designer "Cartoon Network"

THE TALE OF A DRAGON

-1-

It was dark. I was afraid. The darkness, coupled with the dense fog, added to my fear. I didn't know what to expect. The castle walls rose high above me as I made my way across the drawbridge toward the rusted iron gate of the portcullis. I could see green and black moss clinging to the damp gray stones of the castle walls that seemed to grow up out of the murky moat water. What lived in that moat? I remember asking myself as I continued my lonely trek toward the castle gate.

Two flaming torches mounted on the castle wall, one on either side of the drawbridge, were the only lights guiding the meandering crowd into the castle. Those torches, high up the walls, were the only light I could see in the darkness. I continued toward the gate and kept my eyes on those torches – they were the beacons that would direct me into the castle and, though I didn't know it at the time, that path between those bright sentinels was the path to my future.

All I could see was the king sitting high upon the dais. There were two men standing on each side of the throne too – but the center of attention was clearly his majesty, King Edgar. I had never seen a room as big as that throne room. Nor had I seen so many people under one roof at the same time. I didn't even know there was a roof big enough to cover a crowd of that size.

The walls were covered from top to bottom with woven tapestries that depicted stories of great battles and heroic deeds that I remembered from my childhood. One tapestry in particular caught my eye. There was a knight all dressed in his finest armor. Bright sunshine reflected from the polished steel. In the knight's right hand was a fabulous and magical looking sword – a long, straight blade with ancient design forged into the polished steel by the hands of a most skilled blacksmith. A golden pommel on the end of the jewel encrusted hilt revealed the sword as the legendary "Cumhacht", the sword of power wielded by kings since the dawn of time. Cumhacht was the sword held by King Edgar to be passed on to his heir, once he chose an heir. It was well documented that King Edgar had never married and, therefore, had no heir to his kingdom. Why he had never married was not well known and no one seemed willing to ask.

In his left hand the knight held aloft the head of a great, snarling beast. Its eyes were rolled back in their sockets. A long, black tongue lolled from the side of an open mouth. Curved teeth, the length of daggers, showed gruesome, dripping blood and pieces of meat leftover from some newly devoured victim. This was the head of "Laghairt" – the last of the dragons that once terrorized our kingdom – whose lair, legend told was a cave behind Dragon Veil Falls at the far end of Lake Machnamh.

Tales were told of the dragons of old whose powerful wings raised windstorms that warned villagers of the coming destruction. Laghairt's fiery breath and gnashing teeth laid waste to cottages and carried off livestock to be torn and consumed in his cave beneath the great waterfall, Dragon Veil Falls that fills Lake Machnamh. Though it had been decades since Laghairt's death, no man had been brave enough to explore the legendary cave beneath the waterfall – if it truly existed. Someday, I told myself, I would visit those caves, just for the sake of adventure, and to see if they were really there. There were tales of a vast hoard of gold and jewels amassed by Laghairt during his reign of terror. Everyone knew that dragons hoarded great sums of gold and jewels and used their riches as a nest. But, legend also said that dragon treasure was cursed, so no man dared enter the lair of the last known dragon.

-2-

As my eyes continued to scan the great hall there seemed to be a disturbance in a doorway behind the king and his advisers. The doorway was little more than a narrow passage into some hidden antechamber that was partially obscured by a tapestry depicting "Fat" King Egbert riding into battle on his fat horse. Although the story goes that the "Fat" King, who actually went by "Bert", never rode into battle nor did he ride at all since he was so very fat. King Bert never did anything but eat greasy food and drink pots of ale until he fell asleep, face down, at the table. He would awaken there in the morning because he was too fat for anyone to carry up to his bedroom.

In fairness to the royal family, "Fat" King Bert had been the king of a very small and lovely kingdom, our kingdom – Westerford. But, that was many years before. He had been a kind and happy king. His people prospered and felt safe under Bert's protection. But, that was long, long ago when he was married to the lovely Veronica. Queen Veronica was the most beautiful girl in the kingdom. Although she had been born a commoner, King Bert asked for, and received royal permission to marry Veronica. Her hair was blonde as spun gold and the sunlight danced off her golden hair with a sparkle that made it lovelier than any other hair in the kingdom. Her eyes were a deep blue, like a clear spring sky – no clouds, just blue as far as the eye could see. Veronica was tall and slender, with a quick wit and sudden laugh that filled a room with happiness when she was in it.

Veronica and Bert were deliriously happy together. They laughed and sang and told silly tales to one another. Their lovely little kingdom was bright and cheerful and full of life. One winter the king and queen decided to start a family and the next autumn brought forth a bountiful harvest and the most beautiful baby girl the kingdom had ever seen.

King Bert named his daughter Charis. However, on the day Charis was born, tragedy struck the kingdom. In those days, long ago, having a baby was very difficult for mothers. As happened all too often, Veronica did not survive the birth of the princess.

-3-

King Bert was happy with his daughter, but the death of his queen planted a seed of bitterness and sorrow in him that began to grow from the day she was born. The king was no longer the happy fellow he had been when he was young. He grew angry and loud and cruel. King Bert became a buffoon and a blowhard. You might say he was a nincompoop, if anyone knew what a nincompoop was anymore. He always had to have everyone's attention whenever he entered a room. "The King," as he preferred to be called, ate too much, talked too loudly and bragged about things he had done – whether he had actually done them or not.

King Edgar was the brother of "Fat" King Bert. Finally succumbing to his grief at losing Queen Veronica, Bert fell into a long, dark illness, so Edgar took over as King of Westerford. King Bert was no longer able to rule. Bert was reduced to lying in his bed waiting for the end. He was so miserable that he just didn't care anymore.

During his long battle with illness and heartache Bert appointed his brother, Edgar, his heir. Bert also requested that Edgar care for Princess Charis as his own daughter and keep her hidden from the public so that she could grow up without judgment and prying eyes. Edgar was to keep Charis out of the public eye until her eighteenth birthday at which time he could choose a groom for her from any suitor in the kingdom.

Bert's final request was that Edgar test the suitors to find one that was truly right for Charis. He must pass tests for bravery, ingenuity and, most of all, loyalty. Bert created three tasks to be given to any suitor who chose to vie for Charis' hand in marriage. The suitor who successfully completed all three tasks would earn the right to marry Charis and eventually become king. Edgar would remain king until the suitor was properly trained and ready to become king as Bert had once been. When the right king came along the kingdom would once again prosper and rejoice in the happiness it once had enjoyed.

-4-

One summer day, when I was twelve years old, a summons was sent throughout the countryside announcing a general meeting of the entire kingdom in the Great Hall at Westerford Castle. Though still a boy, I was the eldest living male child in my family. My father was in ill health so it was up to me to answer the call. Standing in this giant hall surrounded by representatives from every household in the kingdom was awe-inspiring. In addition to the hundreds or even thousands of people in attendance were the usual knights and ladies of the court. King Edgar was the focal point but it seemed that no one really knew what to expect. The tension was so thick you could cut it with a knife. Not since the transfer of power from "Fat" King Bert to his brother, Edgar, and the hiding away of the Princess Charis, was the kingdom in such a confused state. In fact I had no idea why representatives from every family in the kingdom had been called to the castle. But, as I was the eldest son, and my father was old and had difficulty traveling, it was my duty to represent the family and, young though I was, I never shied away from my duties. King Edgar invited representatives from every family in the kingdom to formally announce the death of "Fat" King Bert and the official ascension to the throne of King Edgar. As one voice the audience shouted, "Long live the King!"

Bert died fat, sad and angry. The kingdom mourned the death of the king as they should. More importantly, the people celebrated his passing with relief because, as Bert had suffered, so had the kingdom. The people remembered with fondness the great king that Bert had been and the happiness and prosperity that everyone enjoyed before the loss of the beloved Queen Veronica.

"Fat" King Bert was not remembered as a good king, but his brother, Edgar was. The people loved him. King Edgar cared about his people. He was neither greedy nor cruel as so many kings could be – at least those kings we read about in history books. Edgar's kingdom was safe. The people had plenty and no surrounding kingdom threatened our borders.

-5-

How do I fit into all of this? My name is Nathaniel. For as long as I can remember everyone has called me "Nat." That nickname first stuck one day when I was about six or seven years old. I was playing in a field near our village with a group of boys and girls about my same age. We were pretending to be knights and we were battling marauders bent on attacking our lands. Of course instead of swords and pikes we had sticks and longer sticks. It was a warm spring day, the kingdom was at peace and we were a bunch of kids playing make-believe. Doing what kids do, and having the time of our lives.

After the first "battle" was over and the good knights had won it was time to choose sides for another round. I asked to be the leader. I had always been fearless, loyal and true. I knew I'd make a fine leader. But, Chase, the blacksmith's son stepped right up to me and said I could never be leader because I was too small. Chase said that I was no bigger than a little bug and that was why my parents named me "Gnat", because I was so very small, like a little bug. I was angry and flew at Chase with everything I had. Chase knocked me to the ground and held me there with his knees on my arms and his big rump on my chest. But, not before my right fist found his belly sending the wind rushing out of him and leaving him gasping for air as he wrestled me to the ground. Chase and I had always been great friends – and would be again in time – but, at that moment, he was no friend of mine. It must have been my tenacity that encouraged the rest of the "knights" playing that day to choose me as their leader. It was true, I was confident and fearless, and, despite Chase's proclamation, the other kids must have seen something in me.

Though my seething hatred for Chase didn't stick, my new nickname did. From that day forward I was Nat. I was often chosen to be leader in our epic, pretend battles, but the name was mine forever. Maybe it was just easier to say than Nathaniel. Maybe it was because, at seven years old, I was not much bigger than a bug.

-6-

As I grew older, I wanted nothing more in the world than to become a knight. But, a knight had to be nobly born and, although my parents were good people, worked hard, and provided for their family, we were not of the noble class. There was only one way for a commoner to become a knight. A commoner could do something "knightly" or heroic and be recognized by the king himself for his heroism. I had never heard of that happening in recent history and couldn't think of a way it could happen for me.

The grains we grew on our farm were used by the king's brewers to make the finest ale in the kingdom. But, even providing grains to the king didn't make my family noble. My mother was kind and gentle with us, and my father worked hard in the fields to provide for our family. Though our house was simple we never wanted for food. We were a close family. My three sisters and I knew that our parents loved us. They taught us right from wrong, they taught us the value of education by teaching us to read, and they shared their love of music and poetry with us. Ours was a happy home. We were encouraged to explore and to use our imaginations, as all children should. Of course we had our chores to do, but once they were done, we were free to roam until nightfall.

Since the odds of me actually becoming a knight were nearly zero I decided that I would simply live my life as a knight would. I would strive to be honest, faithful and brave. I would be loyal to the king and kingdom, study hard to increase my knowledge and I would be ever vigilant – looking for others in need of help and doing whatever I could do to help them. Finally, I would constantly search for true love and commit myself to that love for as long as I lived. If I could not become a knight I figured I could, at least, act like a knight. Because, in my opinion, acting knightly is the only acceptable way to behave.

-7-

My overwhelming desire to become a knight was what had carried me to this particular place in my life. My story was a long and twisted tale that must be told from beginning to end. There I was, at the age of eighteen, once again in the Great Hall at Westerford Castle, kneeling before King Edgar, with the results of my adventure stashed comfortably in my knapsack. I was nervous and unsure as to how this night would end. But, just as that tenacious little boy I once was, playing knights so long ago, I plunged forward asking King Edgar to hear my story without interruption. Imagine that, a lowly knight risen to knighthood from humble beginnings, and through unlikely circumstances, now asking the King not to interrupt my story. Fearless, or crazy? I would discover which soon enough.

-8-

Clearing my throat, I began. "With your permission, King Edgar, I have in my possession evidence of the completion of the three tasks set before me by your highness. If it pleases your majesty I will share the tale of my adventure and the completion of each task in turn. It is my aim that my tale will be both educational and entertaining to the royal family and the rest of the courtiers in attendance."

In his typically boisterous and happy way, King Edgar let out a great burst of laughter, clapped his hands and said, "An entertaining tale of adventure and quest is always welcome in my court. Let the kitchen bring dinner and you may entertain us while we eat."

With that, tables were brought out from the walls and a great feast was spread before us. King Edgar, with a heaping plate of food in front of him drew a long draught from his mug and, wiping his mouth with the back of his hand shouted, "Now, Sir Nathaniel, we shall hear your entertaining tale of adventure and quest. I hope that it concludes with the presentation of relics from the completion of your quest. Nathaniel, the stage is yours. Please, proceed."

"My Lord," I said as I bowed low before King Edgar. "I have completed the quest upon which I was sent and have successfully returned by the prescribed date."

"Rise, Sir Nathaniel, and tell us of your adventurous quest. Entertain us with a story fit for this cold winter night. Include in your story brave deeds, great treasures and acts of nobility worthy of your desired prize," King Edgar said with a smile and a knowing gleam in his eye.

With sweating palms, more than a few butterflies fluttering in my stomach, and a heart full of love and confidence I began, "Highness with the telling of my tale you will see I overcame great danger, discovered a world of amazing treasures and clung tightly to honor and my noble beliefs. May I begin my tale my Lord?"

"I look forward to your tale with great enthusiasm Sir Nathaniel. Please, proceed," said King Edgar.

At the king's command I arose from my seat, pushed my plate toward the center of the table and drank deeply once more from my own mug. I pulled my leather-bound journal out of my knapsack, and looked around at the king and courtiers who waited with eager anticipation for my story. I nodded to the king and began.

"My quest actually began long before I ever arrived here at the castle to approach our great King Edgar about marrying Princess Charis. My tale began long ago, when I was very young. Bear with me as I go back to my childhood so that you have proper background information that will help you better understand how I, a simple man, from humble beginnings, came to rise to knighthood and, with the challenge and blessing of our benevolent king, am blessed with the opportunity to become a member of the royal family and, ultimately, heir to the throne. By the way, becoming heir to the throne was never planned. My love for Princess Charis blinded me to the thought of ruling the kingdom someday."

A murmur of approval ran through the crowd at my last comment. No doubt some in attendance questioned my motives for seeking the hand of the princess. When the crowd hushed again I proceeded with my tale.

-9-

"Your majesty, the directions for my quest were specific in their intended results, but quite general in the methods used to complete each task. I was left to my own devices as far as successfully completing each task was concerned. My Lord said nothing about using outside assistance so long as the individual tasks were completed and the various relics attained. On the table before you I have placed three velvet pillows, one for each of the relics collected on my quest. As my story unfolds many strange and shocking revelations will unfold as well. May I have your word that no one will interrupt my story until I have concluded?"

King Edgar sat back on his throne with a questioning look then burst into laughter once again.

"My boy," the king laughed, "you have my oath that no one, not even I, will interrupt this story. You have my undivided attention and have piqued my curiosity so, that I am ready to burst with wonder. And, once again, I say, please proceed."

With King Edgar's oath and final plea, I opened my leather-bound journal and began my tale.

-10-

"As a young boy, on days when I wasn't playing battles with my friends, I enjoyed exploring the woods by myself. I never wandered too deep into the forest, just deep enough to feel like I was on an adventure. Once, when I was ten years old, I found myself deeper in the old woods than I'd ever been before. Suddenly it seemed to grow colder and darker. Moss grew on fallen and decaying trees. Deep green ferns grew taller than a full-grown man. I wasn't scared, I really wasn't, that is until I was climbing over a fallen tree and crashed through the outer layer of brittle bark, crunch, right into an inky darkness that was cold and damp. The ancient tree was hollow. And I was stuck.

I didn't fall all the way into the tree. Just my head, arms and shoulders broke through. My feet and legs were still kicking on the outside of the hollow tree. Figuring it would be easier to get myself out if I first got all the way into the log, I wiggled my whole body until I slipped right on in. Luckily, moss and decay broke my fall. My landing was rather soft.

As my eyes adjusted to the darkness inside the tree, I began to feel around for a way out. I touched upon something cool and smooth and almost round. It felt a bit like a large serving bowl that had been turned over and buried halfway in the mulch. I tried to lift it but it was stuck. I dug with my hands even though I couldn't see very well. My digging made a shallow trough around the bowl until finally I was able to work it free. It was no bowl, but a sphere of some sort. It felt like an egg, but it was ten times, maybe one hundred times bigger than any egg I'd ever seen before. I had to get it into the light to get a good long look at it. I had to figure out what this egg-shaped thing could possibly be.

I sat down inside the hollow log and pressed my back against one side of the interior. With both legs I could just reach across to the other side of the log. I pressed as hard as I could with both feet, but nothing happened. I stopped to rest for a minute then tried again. This time I thought I heard some cracking and it felt as if the inside of the tree would splinter. Still nothing gave way. I took a much needed break and rested. I reached out and touched the round object to see if it was still there – it was. I had to know what this thing could be. I had to get it out into the light to see if I had stumbled upon some sort of treasure. Again, I leaned my back against the cool inner bark and extended my feet as far as I could to push against the other side of the small tree room I had fallen into. Almost immediately the wall behind me cracked and opened wide spilling me backwards, head over heels onto the soft green forest floor behind me.

As I shook my startled and slightly dizzy head and gathered my bearings I noticed the bowl-shaped object had tumbled out with me coming to rest by my side on a nest of damp ferns. Astonished I realized it was an actual egg – a gigantic greenish-blue egg. At least it was shaped like an egg. What possible creature could come from such a great egg? Certainly it couldn't be a bird of any kind. Bears don't come from eggs nor do the other large animals of the forest. I was curious to the point of needing to know. But how could I find out? I would never break it open to see. That would surely kill whatever was inside. I couldn't take it home with me, people might see it and try to take it from me. Besides when I lifted it I discovered that it was heavy and difficult to move. I decided to bury it under the fallen tree where I found it. I would mark its location and map my steps so that I could find my way back. Once I had my map I would check on my egg everyday and see what happened. What an adventure this was turning out to be.

-11-

Quickly, I looked around making sure I was completely alone. I found a large stick to help me dig a hole underneath one side of the fallen tree. I found an area that was already indented, possibly from when the tree fell years ago. The ground was damp and soft so the digging was easy. Selecting leaves and fern branches, I built a soft nest in the hole for my egg. When I was sure the hole was deep enough and the nest soft enough I rolled the egg into the hole and covered it over with more leaves and fern branches.

I was filthy and exhausted from my labors. But, it was worth it. I couldn't wait to see if my egg would hatch and what kind of creature would emerge when it did. Marking the spot where I made my nest I began the short journey through the forest toward home. It wasn't too far, but I had to keep checking so that I wouldn't forget my way back to my egg.

Every day I eluded villagers and friends to check on my egg. I'd slip into the woods as if I were heading in on one of my childish adventures that I'd taken dozens of times. When I was well into the forest and well out of view of prying eyes, I'd burst into a run until I arrived at my nest. Carefully, I would uncover the nest, examining the egg for cracks or changes of any kind.

Weeks passed and every day, rain or shine, there was no change. Some days I'd remove the covering and just sit for hours staring, watching and wondering when something would happen – or if it ever would.

One day, I had just arrived to check on my egg. The forest floor was damp from the morning dew. A fog rose from the ground and the sun's rays made magical beams, like the sky was raining sunlight through the branches to warm the forest floor. I gently removed the covering from the egg and sat back to watch as always expecting something and, at the same time, expecting the same pang of disappointment I'd experienced every day.

Today was different. Today felt different. Somehow I knew that today was the day I'd been waiting for. But, when would the magic happen? I waited and waited as patiently as ever for a wiggle or a crack. Once again, nothing. It was time to go. Feeling a bit sadder than before, a bit more let down, I started re-covering the nest for another day. Once it was safely covered I turned to make my way home through the forest. Glancing over my shoulder I saw the faintest movement in the branches covering the nest. Maybe it was my hopeful imagination playing tricks on my eyes. But, I stopped to listen and watch.

-12-

Just then it happened. I raced back to the nest and gently pulled away the fern and leaf covering. Sitting back to watch I became witness to something truly incredible. It began with a faint tapping that seemed to come from deep inside the egg. Tap, tap, tap was followed by a scratching sound and the slightest movement – a shift in the egg's position. As the tapping and scratching continued, increasing in volume and intensity, the egg continued to rotate and rock in the nest. More and more vigorous was the motion that I thought the egg would roll right out of the nest.

Then I saw it. The shadow of a line, barely visible at first, as if being drawn from inside the egg, began to show along the outside of the shell. A crack appeared, running the length of the shell from the top, in a jagged line, angling its way to the bottom.

I was shaking with excitement as I watched the egg, my egg, that I'd spent so many countless hours watching, come to life before my very eyes. With a sudden, final crack and an audible pop the egg split in two revealing what appeared, at first, to be a gooey blob of blue-green slime. Exhausted, the creature from within the egg was panting to catch its breath. It stretched its neck and seemed to yawn. Its eyes blinked once, then twice, as it looked at the new world around it. Turning toward me at last and standing on unsure legs to its full height of about twelve inches the creature let out a tiny screeching sound – a combination between a baby's stretching yawn and a happy squeal.

As we made eye contact I nearly tumbled over backward, my mouth fell open and I let out a little scream of my own. I could hardly believe my eyes as, deep in the dense, foggy forest, I found myself face to face with a living, breathing, new-hatched, baby dragon.

I blinked hard and rubbed my eyes trying to clear my head and prove to myself that I wasn't dreaming. There I was, in the misty forest surrounded by green, gray and brown undergrowth, towering ancient, moss-covered trees and the musty scent of forest decay. The normal sounds of the forest seemed to stop as I looked back at the tiny dragon still sitting in half of his eggshell like some pre-historic creature adrift on a pale blue-green boat.

This was no dream and I had to figure out what to do next. I couldn't just leave him here all alone. He was, after all, just a baby. I couldn't really take him home with me either. Baby dragons grow into adult dragons and the other villagers would never allow a baby dragon to survive long enough to become an adult dragon.

Crawling slowly out of his shell, the dragon seemed to sense my confusion and concern. He crept towards me as if to let me know that everything would be alright. He climbed right into my lap and nuzzled me with his head as a puppy would and, instantly, I knew we would be lifelong friends.

I stood up slowly and, lifting the baby dragon in my arms, I made my way to the hollow log where I found the egg so long ago. I lowered the dragon into the tree and climbed in after him. Together we dug a small nest where he could sleep. I lined the nest with leaves and fern branches to give warmth and comfort – the hollow log would provide protection from the elements and anyone who might wander this way in the forest, although I'd never seen anyone else in this part of the forest – as a matter of fact I'd never seen any trace of another person in this part of the forest so I felt in my heart that my new friend would be safe here in his little home.

Once I had his home settled, another question came to mind – what do dragons eat? As I turned to look at the dragon again, my question was answered. A large insect of some sort was creeping along on the inner wall of the log when, without a sound, the dragon snapped it with his powerful little jaws, tipped his head back and with one or two chomps to help it along, swallowed it down. Okay, I thought, relieved, he can feed himself.

Finally, I decided that my new friend needed a name. There was a place I'd heard of in old stories about faraway lands. Danby Wiske was the name of the town in the story. And, although there was never a mention of dragons in the old tales I had always pictured, in my childish imagination, a village where dragons were loved and honored. Danby, in my mind, was a haven for dragons. So, I decided to name my new friend Danby. I looked into his little dragon face and said, "Welcome to the forest, Danby." He looked up at me with a gleam in his eye and seemed to smile a knowing smile. Danby nuzzled me with his nose one last time and then I had to say goodbye for the night. I gave him a hug and told him I'd be back in the morning. Crawling my way out of the hollow log, I turned once more to wave goodbye to my new best friend.

Danby grew quickly. Before too long he was the size of a large dog with wings. While he still fit comfortably inside the hollow log, that's where he made his home. It was a cozy place and it was warm and safe. We were always worried about other people stumbling upon him. At this point nobody knew that there was a real dragon living just a few miles from our village. Worrying about his discovery, I chose different paths every day when I made my treks into the forest to visit and play.

-13-

Danby continued growing steadily and, as he grew, so did our friendship. Legend says that dragons were gigantic, overpowering beasts. In reality, Danby stopped growing when he reached the size of a large horse – a fire breathing horse with wings and a long, dragon tail that is.

We always had fun together, Danby and I. When he was still small we would play fetch with sticks or leather balls. He was fast and agile even when maneuvering through the dense trees of the ancient forest. I would throw the ball as far as I could in any direction I chose and Danby would be off like a flash only to return moments later with the ball securely in his mouth. I also learned that the ball would be more than a little wet from dragon slobber.

As dangerous as it seems, Danby and I would often find a meadow or an open glade where we would wrestle the warm summer afternoons away. We'd romp and tumble in the tall grass until exhaustion overtook us and we collapsed for an afternoon nap.

While it's true Danby could not speak, he could communicate. I soon learned his signals – he would nod, or nudge me or shake his head from side to side. Like a family retriever, he would demonstrate happiness with a wagging tail. When he was naughty Danby would drop his head, put his tail between his legs and slink to my side seeking forgiveness with the innocence of a child.

Once I threw a ball as high into the air as I could throw it. Instead of jumping or waiting until the ball came down to him, Danby gave a great flap of his wings and took off into the sky to catch the ball in his mouth before it reached its highest point. His explosion into the sky was powerful and quick. It was something I'd never seen before and, though I have seen it many times since, the grace and strength he showed was a sight of which I would never tire.

-14-

One day, while we were exploring the forest after Danby had reached his full size, he knelt down and allowed me to climb onto his shoulders. I was riding Danby, a dragon, through the forest as if I was a knight and he was my stallion carrying me nobly into battle. After riding along for several miles we came to a clearing on the edge of a cliff overlooking an enormous body of water. Without hesitation Danby gave a great flap of his powerful wings and we continued right off the cliff and into the sky. My stomach leapt into my throat with a feeling of excitement that I'd never before experienced.

Over the water we soared so low that my toes nearly skimmed the glassy surface. I looked to the side and could see my reflection in the lake with white, scattered clouds for a background. Without notice, Danby turned straight up into the sky, turning like a corkscrew, until we broke through the scattered clouds toward the bright afternoon sun. We flew until the sun's final rays dipped below the horizon. Just as smoothly as we had taken to the sky, we landed back in the clearing with a final flutter of wings and a soft thud of his feet. I had never felt real fear the whole time we were flying, but it felt good to be back on the ground.

Although it was nice to feel the grass and rocks beneath my feet again, all I could think about was getting back into the air and enjoying another flight. Danby and I practiced flying every day. We developed signals to change directions. A small nudge with my left knee and Danby would turn to the right, a nudge with my right knee and we'd turn left. Pressing down gently on his neck with my hands would send us into a dive down to a lower elevation. Leaning back while pressing up with my toes would send us soaring higher into the sky.

-15-

Flying at night time was my favorite. On nights when the moon was full we would soar into the starry sky like a mist drifting on the breeze through a lush green valley. Without a care in the world, Danby and I would circle high above the village, its fires glowing warmly through cottage windows. There was always a faint orange glow at the tops of chimneys where sparks, like tiny fireflies, fluttered into the night. No one ever had a chance to see our village from the sky. It was beautiful in a simple way, during the daytime. But, at night, without the fear of being seen, it was magical.

-16-

One more thing about Danby that proved valuable was his ability to make fire. I'm not sure how it worked, but a deep breath in and a quick exhale with a wide open mouth forced a burst of fire in whatever direction Danby chose. Danby learned to control the fire by regulating the force of the air and by opening or closing his mouth to allow more or less fire to emerge. He could make a fire anywhere no matter how cold it was outside – no more rubbing sticks together or striking flint for me. With Danby and a pile of sticks, we had warmth on cold winter nights or a blazing cooking fire anytime we needed one.

-17-

Most people were frightened of dragons even though they had never seen one. I must admit that the old tales of dragons and their destructive ways were terrifying. Danby was my best friend, the only living dragon, as far as we knew, and would never hurt anyone unless that person tried to hurt me first. Danby didn't steal livestock from farmers nor did he hoard treasure. Once you got to know him there was really nothing about him that was scary. As always, "scary" was the unknown. No one knew Danby even existed but me. Everyone thought the last of the dragons had been slain years ago. It was a mystery that, although everyone believed that dragons were extinct, no one had ever been brave enough to explore the legendary dragon's lair behind Dragon Veil Falls.

It seemed logical to me that some curious treasure hunter or thrill seeker would venture into the cave just to have a look around. If it was true that dragons hoarded treasure, reason would dictate that there would be treasure piled to the ceiling in that cave. Yet no one, as far as anyone knew, would dare enter the dragon's lair behind the falls – if it was really even there. I knew that exploring that cave in search of treasure might be dangerous, but I just couldn't resist the idea of so much treasure. I had no idea what I would do with it if I found a treasure of any real size. As I told myself on that first visit to Westerford Castle, upon seeing the tapestry depicting the slain dragon, Laghairt, I was more interested in the possibility that it might actually exist and the adventure of finding it.

-18-

Dragon Veil Falls created massive whitewater at the far end of Lake Machnamh. The lake was so big that a man could not see from end to end. As a matter of fact, and it will come up again later in my story, now that I've stood in the exact center of Lake Machnamh, a man cannot even see the end from the center of the lake. Dragon Veil Falls tumbles over a jagged rocky cliff to feed Lake Machnamh with fresh mountain runoff from the winter snows in the high mountains. It was in the face of this rocky cliff wall that the dragon's lair cave was said to wind deep into the earth. There was also said to be volcanic activity deep within the cave that, not only made the cave uninhabitable for any living creature except a dragon, but also helped to warm the water of Lake Machnamh. That had to be a myth, however, since Lake Machnamh was not warm at all. People accepted the old stories on faith and without any real proof.

I decided that there must be a way into the cave. Since no one ever dared to venture to that far end of the lake it would be easy for Danby and me to make our way through the forest and right up to the strong cliff wall without being seen.

We set out early one morning before the sun came up. I rode Danby's strong back as he made his way through the dark forest. Dragon's eyes are very similar to cat's eyes in shape and in their ability to see in the dark. I rode along comfortably, confident that Danby had it all under control.

As day broke with the bright morning sun edging its way up above the horizon, I could see a cloud of mist and hear the rumble of the falls crashing onto the rocks below the cliff with a force I had never before witnessed up close. The power of the water was impressive and frightening all at once. It was as if a giant rockslide was tumbling down a mountain without ever stopping. Tons of water made its way violently over the cliff, battering the rocks over one hundred feet below.

Danby and I reached a clearing on the shore just to the right of the falls and a short walk from where the falls entered that side of the lake. As close as we were I began trying to make out the dark outline of a cave behind the falls. With tons of water crashing upon the rocks and waves of mist rising like clouds around the base of the cliff, there was no way to see clearly what may or may not be behind that veil of water. I even asked Danby if he knew how to get into the cave just to see if he had any ideas. He just looked at me with an expression that told me I was on my own.

Giving up thinking I could get a visual on the cave I decided to look for a gap or opening behind the curtain of water. Scanning the cliff wall on either side of the falls, I searched for what resembled a cutout. Before long my eyes locked on a darkened line that zig-zagged the cliff wall and seemed to be a path of some kind that ended about halfway up the falls and disappeared behind the rumbling whitewater. With Danby close behind, I aimed for that line on the wall and made my way around the last bit of lake to where the imagined path began.

Stepping from the edge of the forest my eyes focused on the point on the cliff where I had seen the jagged line on the rocky face. There they were, plain as day, narrow, rocky steps carved into the cliff by unknown masons in a time out of memory. The intricately carved stairway was wet from the waterfall's mist, but it was so meticulously carved that climbing the side of the cliff was rather simple. Standing there in the waterfall's mist, staring up at those steps, I realized that the path was much too narrow for Danby to navigate. It was clear that this entrance was not created for dragons. Danby would have to stay behind at the base of the steps and await my return. I hated leaving him behind as much as he hated being left, that much was clear by the expression on his face. I gave him a quick hug and told him I would be back as soon as possible. I turned then and put my right foot on the bottom step.

Butterflies began swirling nervously in my stomach as the thought occurred to me that I would be the first human being to set foot in the dragon's lair in generations – the first living human being that is. For if legend was true, and dragons were as deadly as the old stories said, there had been many humans in this cave over the years. They just never returned to tell their tale. Climbing those steps, tight against the damp cliff wall was pretty easy going. About fifty feet up the cliff wall, instead of zig-zagging back on itself and away from the falls, the path continued into an indentation and right behind the deafening curtain of water.

-19-

Once I entered the cutout behind the waterfall the mouth of the cave opened to reveal a series of three tunnels leading away from the falls. It was bright enough inside the cave as the sun shone through the falling curtain of water. I was a bit surprised at how bright it was – almost as though sunlight beaming through the great stained windows of a cathedral. The brightness gave me an advantage. Although it would become increasingly darker as I explored the various tunnels that led into the depths of the dragon's lair.

Fortunately, the first tunnel that I started down stopped suddenly, sealed by a smooth rock face that had never opened to a tunnel at all. A false tunnel I decided. Cleaver dragon, I thought. Or was it cut out by the ancient masons that carved the stairway? Of course, the dragons only occupied the cave after it had been carved. A dragon could have no hand in creating neither the finely hewn stairway nor the meticulously carved cave and adjoining tunnels no matter where they led.

One tunnel quickly explored and checked off, two more to go. Instead of rushing to explore the second darkened tunnel, I decided to do a little detective work around the entrances to see if there were any clues. Across the lintel that supported the top of each entrance I could make out deeply carved runes. Unfortunately, I was not able to understand the ancient runic writing so the labeling on each doorway didn't help at all. However, as I inspected the floor in front of each entry I noticed that the central opening showed very little wear. It was obvious that people or animals had passed through that entry, but the passing there had been light and long ago. The third tunnel, on the other hand, had obviously been accessed much more recently, much more often, and the traffic passing into and out of that tunnel was heavy, as if something being dragged back and forth into and out of the tunnel. This third tunnel, I was convinced, had to be the entrance to the dragon's lair.

Creeping slowly down the tunnel was a little eerie even though I was confident that nothing had ventured this direction in many years. A musty smell hung in the air like a cloud and there were not the unmistakable and overpowering aromas of sulphur and death that one would expect to experience upon entering the lair of an active, living dragon. The cave was as dead as the last dragon. And both had been that way for a long, long time.

Keeping to the wall to avoid tripping on fallen debris and because the limited visibility forced it, I was able to make my way fairly quickly through the tunnel. Carved by master craftsmen long ago, the walls and floor were smooth with intricate designs. Even though it had been most recently used to house a dragon, the tunnel was truly a work of art.

Sliding my way along a curve in the wall I sensed rather than saw a glow around the curve in the tunnel. What could possibly be creating a golden glow in a dark, abandoned dragon lair? It must be the dragon's treasure somehow generating a source of light.

As I rounded the final bend in the tunnel the glow grew increasingly brighter until I stopped suddenly and my jaw dropped open at the sight of a gaping roomful of gleaming treasure. Mounds upon mounds of golden coins and jewels of all colors, shapes and sizes reached toward the ceiling. But the richness and beauty of the hoarded treasure was overshadowed by heaping piles of dusty gray bone. I couldn't really tell if the bones were from livestock or humans, but it was obvious that the bones were from meals eaten by previous inhabitants. The bones were as old as the musty air.

-20-

I had found a cave full of treasure. More treasure than any man could ever use. No one had been inside this cave in years nor would anyone venture to enter while the fear of dragons or the legend of dragons hung about. I scooped a couple handfuls of golden coins from the mound, quickly poured them into my knapsack, and hurried out of the dragon's lair into the bright sunshine and cool mist from Dragon Veil Falls.

In an instant I was wealthier than I needed to be. I decided then and there that, if I was ever in a position of power, I would use the riches from the dragon's lair to help all people. Why would I need so much treasure? I'm not a dragon, I'm not greedy, and I don't need to nest on a pile of treasure. This hoard of gold and jewels would make any kingdom the greatest in the world. As I see it, a kingdom is only as great as the quality of life shared by the lowliest people living in it. A leader should be trustworthy, loyal and true. Above all, a leader must take care of his people. Greatness is shared and selfishness leads to a fall from greatness. Someday, I would be a great leader.

For now, I would keep the treasure a secret and share what little I had taken with my family a bit at a time by making small purchases at market. I would use only coins and not jewels so as not to raise suspicions. My parents would appreciate the added income, although they could never know where it had come from. It was not good to keep secrets. But, taking a couple of handfuls of dragon treasure was no crime and keeping the cave behind Dragon Veil Falls a secret was best until the time to reveal the treasure was right.

-21-

The brilliant blaze of the signal fires shone high above the towers. The lighting of signal fires meant only one thing, and that was unusual in our peaceful land. The kingdom was under attack! As the flames were rising from the north towers it was to be assumed that the attack, also, was coming south out of the northern hills. As I wiped the sleep from my eyes and shook the cobwebs from my head, I realized there was something I could do to help. I was only fourteen years old at the time, but with the help of my best friend, Danby, I could put a barrier in front of the invaders to at least slow them down. Danby, after all, was a dragon. He was loyal to me and true to the kingdom, although that had been kept a secret since I found his egg when I was only ten years old.

I raced through the woods as fast as I could, knowing that marauders from the north were coming on fast. How many there were, I had no idea. Our king's guard could fight them off I knew. My only hope was to slow them down to avoid a full midnight attack and possible slaughter. As I closed in on Danby's lair I shouted to arouse him from his sleep and also to let him know it was me approaching. Ready for anything, Danby sprung from his den in the fallen tree where I had found his egg, ducked his head and allowed me to leap onto his shoulders without hesitation.

In an instant we were airborne, soaring through the moonless sky, a mere shadow overhead in the night. Heading north we spotted the invaders crossing the plain on horseback, headed south toward the dry riverbed which marked the northernmost boundary of our kingdom. The riverbed was a natural barrier between Westerford and Comharsa, a sometimes hostile kingdom directly to the north. The bluff on the southern side of the riverbed was crowded with close-growing shrubbery, another natural defense that made it extra difficult for raiders on horseback from Comharsa to invade. Difficult, but not impossible. Approaching enemy forces had to work their way down the northern bluff high above the riverbed and cross the open land that was once a roaring river. After crossing the riverbed, attackers had to climb the southern bluff and fight their way through the wild bushes to reach the inside of our border. It was a formidable natural defense and a surprise attack was really to only way for enemy forces to succeed.

Our troops had not even ridden out of the castle and the enemy was nearing the southern bluff already on our side of the dry riverbed. Without hesitation I urged Danby down to the tangle of brush that covered the bluff. "Fire!" I shouted. Danby knew just what to do. With a deep breath and a mighty blow the brush on the southern bluff exploded into flame as Danby and I flew along the border. The Comharsana were halted in the open bottom of the dry riverbed.

At least until the fire died down the kingdom was safe. King Edgar's guard arrived at the southern bluff just as the fire began to die and the Comharsan horsemen started to rally for another attack up the steep natural slope. It was too late for them. Archers rained arrows on the invaders from above and any riders brave enough to continue the attack were quickly cut down as soon as they crested the southern bluff.

Knowing that our kingdom was safe, Danby and I flew silently back to the forest where we settled into his den for the rest of the night.

-22-

Day broke and Danby and I slept soundly in his cozy den knowing that we had done our part to help save the kingdom from attack. In my mind it was over. We had done all we could do, as any citizen would or should. But, as I entered the village, I soon learned it was not over. Bills were being posted that King Edgar wanted to know who set the fires on the southern bluff.

I knew I was in trouble. With Danby's help, although I'd never give him away, I set fire to one of our kingdom's strategic northern defenses. I was terrified! What should I do? What option did I have? No one had seen me or Danby that night. We were a shadow, a mist in the sky. Only the attackers could have seen us and they certainly weren't talking. I should just keep quiet and tell no one. For as long as I could remember I had been taught to be honest - always. I wouldn't really be lying if I didn't come forward. Lying only counted if someone asked you a question and you gave false information. But then I remembered what my parents always taught me:

Be honest, faithful and true,
Show respect and discipline, too,
No matter what else you do,
No harm shall come to you.

So, without another thought, reciting my parents' rhyme over and over in my head, I began the slow, steep climb up to the castle to turn myself in to the king. Little did I know that short climb would change the direction of my life forever. I had only been inside the castle once before. Of course, every day of my life I had seen the high stone walls rising to the sky like strong cliffs by the sea. Westerford Castle rose before me as I made my way toward the drawbridge that spanned the moat full of mossy green-black water.

No one even noticed me as I made my way through the bustling crowd. I can't say that I'd ever seen so many people in one place in my life. I longed for the quiet and comfort of my village where every face was familiar and everyone knew me by name. I repeated my parents' rhyme as I ascended the vast steps of the great hall and leaned heavily on the giant oaken doors. The doors didn't budge. Just then a mountain of a man, obviously a knight based on his stature and bearing, asked me about my business. I told him that I had come to address King Edgar regarding the fire that burned most of the brush on the northern border. As quickly as I finished my last word, the great doors swung open to reveal the cavernous hall of Westerford Castle. I nervously crossed that threshold for the second time in my life.

-23-

As impressive as the hall was, what truly caught my eyes, just as they had the first time I was there, were the beautiful tapestries that adorned the walls. Each tapestry was a work of art in itself depicting heroes and kings of Westerford. But, the finely embroidered cloth wasn't just a portrait; each tapestry illustrated a heroic scene from Westerford history. I was awe-struck at the sight.

Suddenly, a booming voice jerked my attention back to the task at hand. King Edgar bellowed across the great hall with a voice like thunder, "Come forward, boy, and tell me your name."

In a meek voice I squeaked, "Your majesty, please forgive me. My name is Nathaniel; I live in the village to the north of the castle. I was up late the night of the attack. I saw the signal fires, took a torch and lit the brush on the southern bluff of the riverbed boundary. Please forgive me sire, I thought only to buy time for your guard to arrive and push back the attackers."

I bowed my head deeply, fearing for a moment that the king might chop it off for burning the boundary.

In a voice much softer than before, King Edgar said, "Arise Nathaniel from the village north of the castle."

I looked up and saw that the king held in his hands a medallion of gold on a blue ribbon.

"This is the Cross of Westerford, Medal for Bravery", King Edgar said as he stepped lightly from the dais towards me. "This is the highest, non-military medal awarded in my kingdom. It signifies bravery in the face of great danger, personal sacrifice for the good of others and humility, – which you showed by not seeking attention for your actions."

I trembled as the king approached, placed the medal around my neck and hugged me, kissing both cheeks lightly before turning to return to his throne. I didn't know what to say. I thought I would be in trouble for lighting the bushes on fire. But, I received an award.

"In addition to the medal, the award for bravery is accompanied by knighthood and a place in my royal guard. Return to me when you reach the age of eighteen and I shall bestow those honors upon you as well."

I thanked King Edgar, bowed deeply once more and turned to take my leave. While I retreated swiftly from the hall, I glanced above the doorway and saw a girl about my same age peaking down into the great hall over the stone balcony railing. I thought to myself that she was the most beautiful creature I had ever seen.

"Best to keep your eyes in your head, young man. It's not fitting for a common villager to look too long at the princess," came the whispered voice of the same enormous knight as he opened the door to show me the way out.

-24-

I stepped out of the great hall into the blinding sunlight and suddenly felt lightheaded, almost to the point of falling down. I just had to get back to Danby and tell him what King Edgar had done. When I left him behind in the forest we were both frightened about what kind of trouble I had created. More importantly, we were terrified about what might happen to Danby if anyone found out about him. Leaving him behind in his hollow log home left me with an emptiness that made me feel sick to my stomach. The expression on his face told me that Danby felt the same. What had just happened in the great hall happened so fast that it took me a minute to believe it was true. And I had to share it with my best friend.

Be honest, faithful and true,
Show respect and discipline, too,
No matter what else you do,
No harm shall come to you.

My parents certainly got that one right. But, that vision of beauty overlooking the balcony rail was too much. I turned and looked up to the high castle wall naively trying to catch another glimpse of the princess. There she was, looking down from the battlements with a ring of tiny white flowers encircling her head and wearing an embroidered white dress. The princess was an angel looking down on me. Nervously I raised my hand to wave. She smiled and waved back before turning to leave. And, just like that, my one true love was gone. As I made my way home I walked as if in a dream. It was like I was walking through water, slowly floating along in a stream that carried me back to my village and the quiet peacefulness of my family home.

-25-

As the years passed leading up to my eighteenth birthday, I did everything I could to learn "knightly" skills. But, without the proper instructors or weapons it was difficult. The blacksmith, "Blackie" – most blacksmiths go by the name, "Smitty", but ours was Chase's dad and he was not like other blacksmiths. Blackie was the closest we had to someone who knew about weapons and combat. We begged Blackie long and hard and he finally gave in to making us rudimentary swords and shields.

Chase and I trained like knights, chopping and hacking trees, bushes, pretend enemies and even each other, as we attempted to recreate the mock battles we had witnessed in the king's tournaments. After months of practice we actually were able to handle our swords and shields with passable, if not knightly, form. We both grew taller and our hard training rewarded us with muscles that rippled. I was becoming a man, and in a few short months I would turn eighteen.

-26-

On my eighteenth birthday I would return to the Great Hall at Westerford Castle and King Edgar to be dubbed a knight and made a member of the royal guard. I was sure that it would be too bold of me but, in a matter of weeks, I would also ask the king for permission to marry his niece.

I woke early, long before the sun was up. I washed my face, combed my hair and put on my very finest clothes. Realizing that my "finest clothes" weren't very fine I began to second guess my plan to ask King Edgar for the princess' hand. No, my mind was made up and my resolve firm. If it wasn't to be it would not be for a lack of effort on my part. I would do everything in my power to win the hand of Princess Charis. Nervously, I rode my horse across the well-worn planks of the drawbridge wondering what to expect. It had been four long years since I had crossed that wooden bridge that led through the towering gray stone walls of the castle at Westerford. Had the castle changed? It seemed, somehow, smaller than before. Of course, I was no longer a frightened boy – I was a nervous man, about to become a knight. And, possibly make a complete fool of myself for asking to marry the princess. What quest, if any, would King Edgar place before me? Would Charis even remember me?

There I was, a noble knight-to-be, returning to Westerford Castle where I had been awarded the Cross of Westerford, Medal for Bravery four years earlier, when I was only a boy. That day I arrived to have knighthood bestowed upon me and to lay claim to the princess I'd fallen in love with so many years ago. Though we only shared a brief glance and exchanged shy smiles, I knew my love for Charis would never die. Would

Charis return my love? Would her uncle, King Edgar, consent to our marriage if she did remember me?

Those questions would be answered one way or another that night, I thought. With those thoughts swirling in my mind I looked up and saw Princess Charis looking back at me from her window high in the castle tower.

At first glance Charis' expression was one of surprise and wonder. But, when I looked closer she smiled a happy smile, waved excitedly and turned from the window. Within moments, Charis and two of her attendants were in the courtyard welcoming me with open arms. I was overjoyed! She remembered me, and happily, too. One question was answered. However, I still had to ask King Edgar for Charis' hand in marriage.

-27-

I was provided comfortable rooms in which to wash and rest before meeting with the king at the evening meal. I asked the king's steward, Gregory, to arrange a brief private audience with King Edgar before dinner and my knighting ceremony. He said he would.

Walking down the long hallway to meet King Edgar was the most difficult thing I had ever done. The king put me at ease quickly with his kind smile and welcoming nod. King Edgar remembered my act of bravery that night four years earlier and we briefly retold the story that led to my receiving the Cross of Westerford, Medal for Bravery. Of course, I left out the part where Danby helped make my action possible.

King Edgar was proud to see that I had grown into a strong young man. He said that he was excited to welcome me into his service as a knight and member of his royal guard.

Rising to nobility from common birth was nearly impossible, although it had been done. As a child of fourteen, I had done it. King Edgar had given me an award and an opportunity. He was proud to see that I had made the most of my chance.

After welcoming me back to his castle, the king offered me a seat at his side and asked what was the purpose of our meeting. I summoned all my courage and boldly told the king that his niece, Charis, was the reason for my visit. I told him of my love for her. I explained that I had thought only of Charis since I first set eyes on her four years earlier. Finally, conquering my paralyzing fear, I asked King Edgar for his blessing and permission to court and marry Charis.

Having made my request, I knelt at the king's foot and waited for his reply. King Edgar, in a solemn voice told me to rise so that he could look me in the eye. He smiled and nodded thoughtfully before speaking. I waited breathlessly for his answer. After several forevers King Edgar gave his reply.

"No", he said with an even, steady voice. My heart sank, my head bowed and my eager smile turned to a frown.

"I will not allow you to marry Charis, my only niece and daughter to my brother, Bert, to whom I swore protection as long as I lived. No, you will not marry Charis unless you can earn the right."

The smile rushed back to my face. I knew that, no matter the task, I would win the hand of my beautiful Charis.

-28-

I bowed low, speaking clearly and without emotion. "Whatever your majesty asks, I will do."

King Edgar responded, "I will announce the conditions at tonight's banquet for all to hear, and any who would have the hand of the princess may attempt to meet those conditions. Once you are officially knighted the task will be for you to attempt as well. Until then, you may go."

I walked back down the long hallway with a spring in my step and a smile on my face. I had no idea what the king had in store. I only knew that my future with Princess Charis was within my control.

That evening my appetite wavered as the broad scope and variety of classic quests fluttered around inside my head. I couldn't touch my food even though the king's chef had prepared a feast fit for, well, a king, of course.

Finally, after hours of idle conversation and mindless chitchat, King Edgar rose to speak. At the wave of his hand the dinner crowd was instantly silenced. King Edgar cleared his throat and, in his booming voice, announced:

"My friends and honored guests," he nodded in my direction as he said, "Honored guests." "Tonight begins a most exciting time for our entire kingdom." It has come to my attention that Nathaniel, our noble guest, and newest knight, is interested in marrying my niece, the Royal Princess, Charis. As Nathaniel well knows, Charis is the only child of my only brother, King Bert, may he rest in peace. By marrying Charis, Nat would become heir to the throne of all Westerford."

I realized then, as King Edgar spoke, that his words were absolutely true. I also realized that love truly is blind. I had completely overlooked the fact that, by marrying Charis, I would, one day, become king. My confidence wavered once again, but the moment of doubt passed. Perhaps seeking Charis' hand was too much. I brushed aside the doubts, understanding that, once a gesture of confidence was displayed, it was fatal not to follow through. The fact remained – I loved Charis and would be miserable without her in my life.

"In keeping with my brother, King Bert's, wishes and with an entire kingdom at stake, not to mention my most prized 'treasure', Charis, I have decided that any suitor wishing to compete for her hand in marriage may do so. Each potential suitor must meet several requirements. All suitors must be at least eighteen years old and not older than twenty-five," said the King. "He must be of noble rank no lower than Knight and must have wealth enough to support a family, comfortably, or prospects and the ability to earn such a suitable income. Finally," King Edgar added, "any suitor must successfully complete a series of three, increasingly difficult tasks in order to demonstrate his true devotion to my niece, his skill and bravery as a knight and his nobility as a man. All three tasks must be completed within two weeks' time from the date of the first task. And, of course, the Princess Charis will have final approval of any suitor who qualifies for her hand. However," continued King Edgar, "before any questing or marrying may convene I must ask Nathaniel to please step forward and kneel before the throne and this noble gathering."

-29-

I stepped forward, dropped immediately to my right knee and bowed my head before my king. Edgar drew his sword, Cumhacht, from its scabbard where it hung next to the throne and holding it by the jewel-encrusted hilt, touched first my left shoulder and then my right with the flat of the gleaming blade announcing to the crowd with authority as he did, "In the names of the saints, kings and heroes of Westerford and by my power as King of the realm, I bestow upon you the rank of Knight for bravery demonstrated in the name of our fair kingdom. Rise and be recognized, Sir Nathaniel."

With that I kissed the king's sword, swearing my life and loyalty to the throne of Westerford. Rising to my full height to face the king I felt, at that moment, that I was truly a man and a knight. I had been given a quest, the details of which were vague at best. Suddenly, and for the first time, my life truly had meaning.

The final words King Edgar spoke during his announcement were the words I held onto as I wrote my name on a piece of paper, thus declaring my intent to marry Charis, and slipped it into the box near the great oak doors at the entrance to the hall. I knew, in my heart, that Charis would accept me if I could meet the rest of the requirements prescribed by the king.

My recent elevation to knighthood on my eighteenth birthday covered the first two requirements and my discovery of the mound of treasure behind Dragon Veil Falls gave me wealth enough to provide for all the families in the entire kingdom. It would come down to completing the three tasks in two weeks. What would the tasks be and would I be able to accomplish them within the two-week time limit?

As Gregory, King Edgar's steward, handed me three small envelopes and wished me good luck with a wink and a smile, I knew I'd discover my future soon enough. Each envelope was numbered and imprinted with the words: "Do not open until the previous task has been successfully completed."

-30-

The next morning I was sent to see the king's blacksmith and armorer to be fitted for a sword, a shield, and plate armor and chain mail. In no time at all I was a true knight in title and appearance. Soon after receiving my sword, shield and armor, the time came for me to take my leave of Westerford Castle and begin my quest.

-31-

I tore open the envelope marked "Task #1" that Gregory, the king's steward, had given me. Inside the envelope was a small piece of paper. On the paper was written the instructions for my first task:

Task one is a challenge
That most men can crack,
Just climb to the top of a
Mountain and back.
In a cave on Mount Uasal
Rests a jewel of renown,
No finer treasure on earth
Can be found.
Place the 'Eye of the Mount'
In the palm of my hand,
Then I will possess the
Best jewel in the land.

-32-

The chill wind burned my face as it swept across the packed ice and snow. Though the sun shone brightly through scattered clouds, it was cold. Mount Uasal was tall. It wasn't as high as the mountains in faraway countries that I heard about in stories when I was younger. But, Uasal was the tallest ever seen by the people of our kingdom.

Still I began to question why I was climbing this mountain to complete one of King Edgar's three tasks. No other man in the whole kingdom had come close to retrieving the "Eye of the Mount" from the cave high atop Mount Uasal. Completing the three tasks seemed impossible so most men didn't even try. King Edgar promised the hand of the princess to whomsoever completed all three tasks. King Edgar was such a wise and virtuous king and I was looking for an opportunity to serve him any way I could. Marrying the princess or not, I could complete a task or two in the name of King Edgar. It would be my honor. Now that I was on the side of Mount Uasal, blinded by sunlight glaring off packed snow crystals like a million tiny mirrors, my desire to honor the king began to waiver. My love for Charis, however, did not.

Suddenly, a beating sound came to my ears. Was it my heart beating loudly from sheer exhaustion? Or was it something I'd grown familiar with since that foggy morning in the woods near my home so many years ago? I waited and peered into the blinding sunlight for a brief moment until a black spot in the middle of the white noonday sun grew into the shape of my dear friend, Danby.

That silly dragon – I told him to stay in his hollow tree in the woods, out of sight. I would complete task number one on my own or it wouldn't be completed. At least it wouldn't be completed by me. But here was Danby, to the rescue. Gliding low over the snowpack, he landed behind an outcrop of rock just ahead and waited for me. I smiled and patted his nose when he shyly dipped his head to ask forgiveness. I thanked him and hugged him around the neck. Then I climbed into position with my knees in front of his strong shoulders and my feet hooked behind his wings – I guess you'd say my toes were in his armpits. Danby never seemed to mind before and he didn't mind now. That grip made me feel safe and secure as his powerful wings drove skyward and we began circling the top of Mount Uasal searching for the elusive cave and, ultimately, the "Eye of the Mount," which was tucked safely inside the cave. But, where was the cave? And, once inside the cave, where would I find the "Eye"? There are never signs or roadmaps for hidden treasure.

Danby and I circled slowly about the top of Mount Uasal. Keeping low and using rocks and trees as natural shields from prying eyes we tracked a path round and round the mountain, working our way systematically back and forth trying to locate a dark, yawning cave opening. Then it suddenly dawned on me that perhaps the cave wouldn't be a dark opening, but a white, reflective, ice cave. I realized we were looking for the wrong kind of cave and I knew just what to do. I gave Danby a nudge with my toes and told him to climb directly toward the morning sun. When we reached what I thought might be high enough I signaled that we should begin a dive back toward Mount Uasal. As we turned our backs to the sun and began our descent we saw it almost at once. A flash of brilliant reflection caught our eyes, blinding us for a moment, like a beacon guiding the way to a mirrored entrance to the hidden cave on Mount Uasal.

Danby landed softly though the snow was packed hard around the narrow cave opening. I slipped from my spot on his strong shoulders and made my way toward the entrance. Danby gave me a look of encouragement mixed with worry as

I glanced back. I asked him to wait for me and he stamped his foot and nodded as if that was a silly question. I was just being a bit nervous and Danby was being reassuring in his own way.

-33-

I had to turn sideways to enter the cave. It was like sliding between two huge panes of shiny glass – I would say mirrors, but the ice was so clear I could see many feet through it before the view was broken by cracks and grainy whiteness. The cave was truly magical. Although it was cold inside I never felt danger or true fear. No one and nothing appeared to have been in the cave for many years. Who knows when was the last time anyone had even found the opening.

After passing through the opening, making my way sideways through the long entrance, I slipped into a giant chamber. There were brilliant colors reflecting from the ice walls. The tiny amount of sunlight that made its way into the chamber from the outside world danced and glinted from every surface, making a light display not seen before or since. It was incredible and minutes passed before I realized I was standing alone in an ice chamber on Mount Uasal mesmerized by dancing lights with my mouth wide open.

Snapping my mouth shut, I began to look around for signs of the object of my visit: the "Eye of the Mount."

A cave of mirrors surrounded me. It was like I was tiny and crawling around in broken glass. Some of the ice reflected and some I could see right through. It was eerie and beautiful and strange all at once. All of a sudden I saw it. In the heart of the giant ice cave, surrounded by enormous tooth-like icicles, on a pedestal of carved ice that looked like hand-blown crystal, was the "Eye of the Mount." I'm not really sure what I expected. There was no description given. I figured I'd know it when I saw it. I did. In a cave of ice reflecting blue and white with glimmering sun sparkles throughout, the "Eye of the Mount" stood out as the most perfect jewel I certainly had ever seen. It was large and shaped like a diamond the size of the giant pine-cones we used to find in the forest. It was clear with a hint of blue – I was told later that it was a sapphire, though not dark blue like most sapphires. The "Eye of the Mount" was the color of the crystal ice cave where I found it. Reaching out, I gently took the gem from its pedestal and quickly slipped it into my knapsack.

Suddenly, and all around me, the walls began to rumble as if an avalanche were crashing straight through the narrow entrance to the crystal cave – now I was afraid. The icicles hanging from the ceiling began to sway, gently at first, then with more violence until one by one they began to drop from where they hung like crystalline spears being thrown from above. Without looking back I ran to the entryway and slipped sideways out of the cave. Danby was there to greet me and I'd almost swear he was smiling as I patted his neck, panting with relief, and took my place on his strong, safe shoulders.

As we lifted into the clear morning sky, heading for Danby's lair in the forest I wondered how I would complete task number two. The first of three tasks completed, the "Eye of the Mount" safely in my knapsack, I closed my eyes to feel the wind in my hair and the sun on my face. My best friend and I soaring home to rest. I had plans to make.

-34-

When we landed softly back in the forest, I was so excited that I decided to open the envelope for "Task #2" right then and there. The slip of paper inside the envelope read:

The heart of Lake Machnamh
Holds a pearl round and pure,
The greatest the sea can produce
To be sure.
Use caution and care,
Bring the great pearl to me,
In my hand you will place
The fair "Moon of the Sea.

Finding the "Moon of the Sea" at the bottom of Lake Machnamh would not be easy. But, to win the hand of Charis, as King Edgar announced, I surely could find a way to lay the "Moon of the Sea" into his hand next to the "Eye of the Mount."

First rest, then food, then a plan.

My bed, although really only a rough cloth cover stuffed with straw, had never felt so comfortable. I dreamt of that icy mountain, the crystal ice-cave reflecting like a thousand mirrors, and my narrow escape as the cave collapsed behind me. But, mostly, I dreamt of flying on Danby's back, the wind in my face, the rush of rising and falling on the powerful dragon's wings.

-35-

As King Edgar said, task one was pretty easy. Although climbing the icy mountainside was difficult, the task could have been accomplished by almost anyone. Of course having Danby certainly helped since actually finding the ice cave without Danby's help would have taken days. By the time anyone not using a dragon as an assistant, which would be everyone else trying to find the ice cave, actually found the cave, I would be well on my way to completing task number two.

Discovering the "Moon of the Sea" in a dark cave in the heart of Lake Machnamh? How would I ever be able to complete task number two?

Getting to the heart of the lake would be a trick. It must be very deep and dark and cold. I know Danby can dive deep into open water. He often fishes in the deep waters off the coast when forest animals are difficult to come by. Danby never steals from local farms or villages. I warned him long ago that the less people saw of him, the less people would fear him. And, fear is what drives humans to want to destroy dragons.

Since I knew Danby could swim, all I had to do was figure out how he could take me with him into the heart of the lake and back without me drowning. Oh, and find the cave and the pearl all in one underwater trip. This task would be a challenge, one that I wasn't sure anyone could complete.

As I stood on the foggy shore of Lake Machnamh looking over the smooth, glassy waters that reflected the ancient forest and snowcapped mountains that surrounded it, I imagined the "Moon of the Sea" in its cave deep beneath the crystal waters. I wondered how, even with Danby's help, I could ever dive deep enough to locate the pearl in the cave at the "heart" of the lake.

Suddenly it dawned on me that the "heart" of the lake didn't have to mean deep, it could simply mean "middle."I called to Danby who had been hiding in the edge of the forest, among the shadows of the ancient trees, well out of sight of wandering eyes. His deep blue-green scales blended nicely with the colors and shadows of the wild forest. As he crept slowly from the shelter of the trees I told him that I thought the "heart" of the lake might actually be the center, not the bottom. I asked him to fly me over the center of the great body of water to see if there was a sign that my hunch might be right. Danby nodded and stamped his foot in approval. He lowered his head and shoulders so that I could climb into my "pilot's" seat behind his great shoulders. Sitting there on Danby's back was always thrilling. The anticipation of flying was never boring – no one in the kingdom or the whole world could claim to ride a dragon. That freedom was mine alone. The opportunity I had to fly through the sky with my very best friend was one I would never take lightly.

We flew low out over Lake Machnamh. Skimming the surface of the clear, dark waters I could look down and see the reflection of my great friend with the blue sky for a backdrop and wispy, white clouds accentuating the vision. It was beautiful and liberating all at once. As we approached the center of the lake I leaned back indicating that Danby should rise higher into the sky to give us a better view of the lake. We rose on powerful wings and banked to the left, circling the center counter-clockwise. My stomach churned as it always did when Danby tipped to the side. But, I knew I was safe. I knew Danby would never let anything happen to me.

As we banked, I could see over my left shoulder what looked like a light patch of water in the center of the dark lake. I shouted for Danby to make for the patch and he tilted his wings diving toward what I quickly saw was a small, barely submerged, island – most would call it nothing more than a sand bar.

Circling closer I could see that right in the center of the island was a hole. This must be the cave entrance I whispered to myself. The sand island looked to be no deeper than four or five feet so I asked Danby to land on it near the hole in the center. We touched down with a gentle splash and the water barely touched my feet as the wind-swept ripples lapped at the dragon's chest. With slight pressure from my knee, Danby eased over toward the large hole in the center of the island. An oxcart could easily drive right into the cave, if you could get oxen to pull a cart straight down into the water in the middle of a lake. We didn't have oxen or a cart. It was just me and my best friend. I slid from Danby's back. The cool water came nearly to my shoulders. Danby looked concerned. I felt concerned, but tried not to show it. I was on the verge of completing task number two of King Edgar's glorious quest.

-36-

I took a couple of deep breaths, filling my lungs deeply with fresh air and then letting it out again. On the third breath I doubled over in the water and dove as quickly as I could through the opening and down as deep as I could dive. I held my eyes open but could barely see. The water was clear enough and it was fresh lake water so it didn't sting like the salty ocean water I'd swam in many years before. But, it was dark in that cave. As I reached a depth of about ten feet, with the pressure building in my head and chest, the opening began to bend to the right. I swam along the floor with one hand touching the wall. Inching my way along, cautiously but as quickly as possible, I could feel the floor begin to rise. Suddenly, unexpectedly, I broke through the surface of the water. Treading water in the darkness I gasped for air as I tried to gather my bearings. There was a stale, stony taste to the thick air. But, at least there was air and I had found my way into the "heart of the lake."

I still couldn't see very well, although my eyes were slowly adjusting to the darkness. There must have been a tiny bit of light making its way through the underwater passage into what I realized was a submerged cave – a large pocket of air and a small island allowed me to catch my breath and rest from my short, but terrifying swim. I looked around in the dim light of the cave and there, on a pedestal of what seemed to be polished stones, carved and stacked tightly the way the ancient engineers built their temples, with no need for mortar, was a great pearl larger than a knight's fist. Though the cave was mostly dark, the pearl, the "Moon of the Sea," shone with a luminescence that could only come from deep in the ocean.

I lifted the pearl and held it in the palm of my open hand. The weight and balance of the pearl were perfect. I was no expert in the true value of pearls, although I had seen merchants asking a pretty price for them at market. The pearls I had seen were much smaller and not nearly as lustrous as the "Moon of the Sea." Knowing the asking price of the smaller pearls in the marketplace, the density and color of the great pearl in my hand made this treasure priceless. Truly a gift from the sea gods, this jewel would make King Edgar burst with pride. Task number two was nearly complete.

I took two more deep breaths of the thick air in the underwater cave. As I pulled the musty air into my lungs, I slipped the "Moon of the Sea" into my knapsack, took a third and final breath and slipped back into the cool water. I followed the same tunnel that led me to the pearl. Fortunately, there weren't any other tunnels to lead me astray to a watery grave. As I turned the same corner I'd found on the way in, I looked ahead up the tunnel and could see the light of the blue sky framing the face of my friend. He'd waited for me, standing in the cool lake water up to his chest, staring into the mouth of the cave probably wondering if I'd ever return. As I broke the surface of the lake, gasping for fresh air, Danby grabbed me with both arms in a tight dragon hug. I was happy to see him and moments later even happier to be astride his shoulders soaring toward the safety of the forest, rest, food and the completion of task number two.

-37-

That night I rested with the deep sleep of someone who had accomplished a goal. I had met a challenge and succeeded. I would place the "Moon of the Sea" into King Edgar's hand. What could task number three possibly be? The second task was more difficult than the first. So, it was safe to assume that task three would be even more difficult yet. I left Danby asleep in his forest home and, with a spring in my step, walked to the village. I entered the public house and sat down at one of the old wooden tables. With the appetite of an adventurer, I ate a large breakfast of eggs, ham, potatoes and fresh bread with jam. I was famished and the meal was delicious. When I finished my breakfast I decided it was time to open the envelope marked "Task #3." As I read the directions for task three my heart sank and I nearly wept. There was no way I could imagine successfully completing task number three:

Task three is the hardest,
You'll know when you've won.
Your worth will be proven,
It's never been done.
Search high and low,
'Cross the land and the sea.
When you find what you seek,
Bring it back here to me.
There's no prize so great,
But no prize if you fail.
Do not return without
A dragon's tail.

-38-

Two weeks had passed since I had undertaken the King's challenge that would earn me the right to marry Princess Charis. I dressed for my ride to the castle and my meeting with King Edgar. Feeling a bit more nervous than I had for my previous meetings I mounted my horse and rode through the forest toward the castle. The "Moon of the Sea" was safely tucked away in my knapsack next to the "Eye of the Mount" and my sword hung at my side for protection. Oh, and Danby, of course, followed at a distance using his keen sense of hearing to protect me from thieves. As expected there was no trouble on the forest road. I was familiar and a knight. No one knew that I carried treasures of immeasurable value in my tattered old knapsack.

Danby waited in the forest as I broke into the bright sunlight from the darkness of the forest road. Westerford Castle loomed in the distance, multi-colored pennants waving in the morning breeze from the top of the battlements. Sunlight reflected from the moat's mossy green water as I made my way across the worn drawbridge and into the castle yard where I dismounted, handed my horse's reigns to the squire who ran out of the stable to assist me, and made my way toward the Great Hall and King Edgar. As I entered the hall, I looked up at the tapestries on the wall and envisioned myself up there one day – a hero of the kingdom and, potentially, a future king. A chill of sadness swept over me as I realized those things might never happen.

-39-

When I first mounted the steps that led up to the massive oaken doors, I had no idea what I would say or where I would even begin. My story was a long one and, as far as I knew, it was now ending in failure. On the other side of those doors awaited my fate. King Edgar, our leader, our benevolent ruler, was expecting me to return with the third, and final, task complete. But, try as I might, I just couldn't bring myself to complete my task. I, indeed, had failed. And then it struck me. I had already completed task number three. The completion of my quest was already in my possession and all I had to do was deliver it to King Edgar.

With a newfound confidence I entered the Great Hall prepared and excited. Walking toward the King with my head held high, I was revived, and I had not failed. King Edgar would know that I was loyal and true, trustworthy and brave. The hour was mine and I would deliver. This was the night that I would earn the right to marry the princess and, although it was not by design, become heir to the throne and protector of the kingdom. Feeling a deep sense of honor and humility I made my way toward King Edgar. I stopped short of the dais and bowed deeply to show the level of love and respect I had for my king. When Edgar signaled that I should rise I straightened my back and stood tall and proud as a true knight should.

-40-

Finding the "Eye of the Mount" was the simplest of the three tasks. The "Eye" represents observation, focus and intelligence, and it took all three of these to discover the secret to where the "Eye" was hidden. Using my ability to focus all of my energy on the task at hand helped me to observe the signs around me. I asked questions of myself to eliminate false leads; I narrowed all possible options by crossing off where it couldn't be, until I found the hidden ice cave and, ultimately, the "Eye of the Mount."

A collective gasp of awe ran through the crowd as I withdrew the "Eye" from my knapsack and placed it gently on its blue velvet pillow on the king's table.

"I lay before you, King Edgar, from the depths of a hidden ice cave atop Mount Uasal, a symbol of intelligence, observation and focus, the legendary 'Eye of the Mount.' May its power and beauty bring clarity of judgment and humility of perception to your house from this day forward."

-41-

"Symbolizing cycles of the seasons and life, and representing intuition and common sense, the 'Moon' is often shadowed in mystery. Finding the 'Moon of the Sea' in the heart of Lake Machnamh took all of my powers of perception. It would be humanly impossible to either place the 'Moon' at the bottom of the lake or to eventually retrieve it from such depths. As the moon represents time, it is only through time that a pearl develops. It was also through time that I was forced to find balance between my emotional desire to quickly find the 'Moon of the Sea' and the intellectual, time consuming, progression it takes to understand that the 'heart' of the lake did not have to be at the bottom. We understand that the human heart is at the center of the body just as the 'heart' of the lake was at the center of the lake."

Everyone in attendance leaned forward and King Edgar nearly fell from his throne as I reached into my knapsack and pulled from its depths the "Moon of the Sea," placing it gently on a pillow of black velvet next to the "Eye of the Mount" atop the king's table.

"May the 'Moon of the Sea' create a balance in your kingdom between emotion and intuition. May your reign be filled with wonder and illumination. And, may your majesty influence generations with perception and progressive thinking."

-42-

"Finally, strength, courage and honesty are all represented by the dragon in stories passed down from generation to generation. From early childhood we are told of olden times when fierce dragons ruled the skies and countryside terrorizing villagers by destroying crops, stealing livestock and hoarding treasure in their secret lairs. Were they the stuff of legend and fantasy? Were dragons created in the minds of the kings long ago to give battle-trained knights a noble quest during times of peace?"

"Dragons, historically, also symbolize luck, loyalty and brotherhood. As my story has unfolded before you it is obvious that I could never have accomplished my quest without my loyal companion, Danby. I consider him a brother in the truest sense of the word. He is noble, patient and true. Danby is neither jealous nor spiteful. He has strength beyond measure and courage to support me without question or concern for his own safety. Danby, the only dragon left in the whole of the world, has never harmed one human, has never terrorized villagers, or stolen livestock from simple farmers. Danby has helped me on my quest so that I might win the hand of the beautiful Princess Charis.

Your Majesty, King Edgar, I present to you, Danby, loyal and humble friend, protector of the kingdom and main character of my tale, which I now present as the third, and final, relic of my quest – The Tale of a Dragon."

With that I closed the leather-bound journal from which I had been reading and laid it gently on the third velvet pillow resting lightly on King Edgar's table. The title imprinted on the ornate leather cover read: "The Tale of a Dragon."

There was a silent pause throughout the hall while the whole court tried to read the look on the king's face. I bowed low before Edgar awaiting some response. Finally, after a seeming lifetime of waiting, King Edgar jumped to his feet, erupting in laughter and applause triggering a greater eruption from the entire hall of people who had witnessed my story.

-43-

With a wave of his hand King Edgar silenced the wild crowd and with tears of joy and a genuine smile he shouted,

"Bravo, Sir Nathaniel! A more entertaining tale of adventure I have never heard before."

The crowded hall murmured wildly and nodded their agreement as one.

"You have learned much from your adventures and grown into just the kind of knight I want to lead my Royal Guard. You are brave, loyal and honorable. You have displayed intelligence, creativity and vision. You have overcome obstacles that would confound many of the most courageous knights, shown intuition and common sense where many learned scholars would stumble. But, perhaps most importantly, you have remained a true and loyal friend. Though your undying loyalty could have resulted in failing to complete your quest, you held fast to your values and trusted deeply that I would demonstrate the same qualities in my judgment of your tale. From this day forward the symbol of the dragon shall appear on my standard to depict strength, power, courage, honesty and loyalty. A tapestry depicting your valiant quest shall be commissioned to adorn the walls of my great hall for all to see who enter here for judgment or entertainment. And, finally, you shall marry my niece, the Princess Charis, making you heir to the throne of all Westerford, and future king. May your marriage be noble, faithful, honest and fruitful. May you reign over the land with intelligence, compassion and honesty for as long as you shall live. May your kingdom dwell in peace and prosperity as long as you shall reign and may you lead through your example of what is good and right and just in the world."

-44-

Just then we heard a sound from outside. It was a sound like trumpets on a wind. I rushed to the terrace overlooking the courtyard to see Danby gliding toward the opening near the castle. King Edgar and the rest of the courtiers stepped back in awe, but I moved toward Danby with a confidence that he was my true friend and that I had nothing to fear. Danby landed with a soft thud and a final flap of his great wings. I walked to him and wrapped my arms around his muscular neck as he nuzzled me affectionately with his nose.

King Edgar approached cautiously with a look of wonder on his face. I stepped back and said,

"Your Majesty, King Edgar of Westerford, this is Danby, the true and noble hero of my tale."

Danby bowed deeply toward the King, and Edgar smiled and nodded his approval of Danby.

"From this day forward, Danby the Dragon shall be a welcome citizen of Westerford. He will live under my protection as long as I rule."

A cheer from the mesmerized crowd of onlookers began to rise into the clear night sky. In response, Danby leaned back his head, took a deep breath and blew a fireball into the clear night sky that is recalled, to this day, as the greatest firework ever seen over the kingdom of Westerford.

Charis and I were married in a forest clearing on a beautiful spring day with birds singing and flowers blooming. The whole kingdom was in attendance including my best friend, a Dragon named Danby.

THE DRAGON KNIGHTS OF WESTERFORD

-1-

In the weeks that followed the wedding, life was grand. Charis and I were having the time of our lives. We traveled around the kingdom visiting all the villages along the way. The days were sunny and the people we met on our travels were beyond friendly and welcoming. Although most of the villagers had very little material wealth, as was fairly common throughout the world that we knew, they were happy just working the land in peace. In return King Edgar ensured that everyone had work and that no one ever went hungry. A solid day's work was rewarded with a place to call home and plenty of healthy food on the table. This was the way of our kingdom established by "Fat" King Bert during the joyful days before he lost his wife, Queen Veronica. Things were so happy and prosperous in those days that King Edgar adopted the same policies when he succeeded his brother, Bert, the Fat King.

After the passing of King Bert, Edgar restored the kingdom quickly to happiness and prosperity, which was the way I had always known the place I called home. Ruling the kingdom would one day be my responsibility. Meeting the people and learning the history and geography of Westerford all were woven into my daily training.

Of course, the villagers had heard news of my marriage to Princess Charis. And everyone knew that I had earned King Edgar's blessing to marry Charis by successfully completing the king's three tasks. My "Tale of a Dragon" was the talk of Westerford. In the villages we visited throughout the kingdom, we saw children at play and it seemed that every little boy wanted to be Nat and every little girl wanted to be Charis. A large dog or a small pony usually played the role of Danby.

Word had reached the people that it was Danby who actually set the fires on the border to help defeat the attackers so many years before. The villagers started to reconsider their feelings toward dragons. After all, they conceded, they had not actually seen a dragon for many years and this one had been living in the nearby woods for a long time without once stealing their livestock or terrorizing their villages.

There was an old saying that went: "You never really know a person until you climb into their skin and walk around in it." Maybe dragons were shy and lonely and just wanted to make friends but no one would take the time to get to know them.

Danby, Charis, and I were invited to visit every village throughout the kingdom. Every festival, no matter the reason for the celebration, included our introduction and the awarding of some ribbon, medal, plaque or trophy. And, of course, with each celebration came plenty of food. The warmth we felt was genuine and generous. We had earned a special place in Westerford and could never repay that love with a thousand quests – although, certainly, we would try.

-2-

My tale and quest changed my life, and it also changed the kingdom. Danby became an instant celebrity. As crazy as it seems, we were heroes. King Edgar even vowed to add the dragon symbol to his banner as a pledge to Danby that he was forever a welcomed citizen of Westerford.

After our wedding Charis and I moved into a series of rooms in the east wing of the castle. This part of the castle had been the personal chambers of King Bert and Queen Veronica during their happy years together. The rooms had remained sealed, unused and forgotten since Veronica's untimely death. A thorough cleaning by the house staff and the east wing was, once again, the happiest place in the castle.

The walls were painted with detailed forest scenes depicting trees and flowers, birds and animals. Brightly colored murals and oversized, comfortable furniture decorated the rooms. Charis had never been in the east wing as it had been closed off when she was a newborn baby. She had no childhood memories of the rooms so it was as if a new wing had been added to the castle just for us.

True to his word, King Edgar made Danby a valued member of Westerford. The kingdom's flag was altered to include a great winged dragon flying across the already green background with Mount Uasal reflected in the clear waters of Lake Machnamh.

The king also had built a fine "lair" for Danby. Rather than giving Danby a room in the castle or building a wooden structure for a house, Edgar designed a special "cave" for Danby beneath the castle walls with easy access to the Westerford courtyard. Danby's home was clean and dry. The floor was strewn with fresh hay and he could come and go as he pleased, always with the protection of the great castle's high stone walls.

Although he couldn't tell me with words, the expression on his face told me that Danby was happy. He had a home. We were together daily and could journey wherever we liked now that Danby was no longer my secret. And, he could hunt in the forests and waterways when he was hungry without fear of prying eyes.

Needless to say, our lives had changed for the better. From our secret childhood in the forest to new homes in the castle and a future as bright as the sunshine on a Westerford spring day. Life had turned magical.

-3-

As if my regular training as a knight wasn't enough, I was assigned a tutor to educate me in many areas important to my role as heir and future king. My tutor, Ollamh, was kind and funny, but he was strict. Ollamh was very old with long white hair that blew in the wind like the stringy mane of my father's old plow horse. He wore dusty robes tied at the waist with a length of rope and a silly, floppy muffin hat that fell limply to the side of his head. The hat had a large feather that stuck out from the side. Only later did I learn that the feather was actually a quill ink pen that Ollamh kept in his hat in case he suddenly needed to scribble some notes. Ollamh's white beard was as wispy as his thin hair and hung down well below his flat stomach. He was tall and surprisingly fit for an old man, probably because he walked everywhere he went carrying a long walking stick that was polished smooth from countless years of use.

Ollamh taught me many things. Unlike most people my age who had grown up in a small country village, I could already read and write. My parents were not wealthy, but they knew the importance of an education even if one was going to be a farmer or a blacksmith. It was important to my parents, long before my surprising rise to knighthood that I should be a well-rounded adult so they made me learn. Reading and writing became the cornerstones of my new life of learning and training, and I could thank my parents for giving me a head start.

Ollamh also taught me history and geography. Knowing the history of Westerford was of extreme importance. I learned about previous kings and how they came to power, whether by blood or by marriage. Part of that history focused on the qualities that made a good king: leadership and loyalty, honesty and intelligence. I discovered that a truly strong ruler was not just a great warrior, but also someone who could see a problem from many different sides and choose, wisely and rationally, the best way to deal with that situation. Sometimes the only way to solve a crisis was war. But, even more often, the right choice, the wise choice, the "kingly" choice was peace – even if that meant giving in to your opponent in certain areas to maintain that peace.

I studied geography by learning the boundaries of our kingdom and the natural landmarks within those boundaries. I also learned the geography of the surrounding kingdoms. Ollamh taught me which kings were friendly and which kings would like to take over part of our kingdom, if they could. Fortunately, most of the countries bordering ours were friends and allies. We shared long-standing peace agreements and traded regularly with each other. Our kingdom, I learned, was truly happy. We enjoyed prosperity and wealth without the need to over-tax our people. King Edgar was wise, generous, and joyful. The people were content too. Everyone in Westerford knew that King Edgar had never been married. Before he became king, Edgar had been in love with a beautiful woman with flowing red hair who lived somewhere in Tranglam Forest. Ollamh told me that there was a long story behind the king's lost love and, perhaps someday, he would tell me the sad tale.

-4-

"I need to let you in on a little-known secret, Nat," said Ollamh. During our game of chess, as was often the case, we discussed Westerford and its surrounding kingdoms. My ears perked up at the thought of secrets and I leaned forward to hear more as Ollamh slid his bishop across the board putting my queen in jeopardy.

"You see," Ollamh continued as I scanned the board trying to think of my next move while waiting to hear Ollamh's secret. "Westerford is surrounded on three sides by lesser kingdoms and on the fourth side by a vast ocean. Our kingdom has been at peace for many, many years. Word has come to King Edgar that two of our neighboring kingdoms, especially Comharsa to the north, have begun preparations for some sort of invasion," Ollamh said as I slid my rook to block his bishop, thereby protecting my queen.

With the word "invasion" my interest in chess waned and Ollamh had my undivided attention. Although, in a way only Ollamh could, he focused more intently on the board in front of him, analyzing each piece before deciding on his next move. In a dusty, almost bored voice, Ollamh said, "King Edgar has decided to create a small team of highly trained knights to patrol and observe what he calls the 'hot' borders between Westerford and the neighbors in question." Sliding his bishop one square Ollamh added, "Check."

I grinned at the subtlety of his move and asked, "Do you think the king has anyone in mind to lead such a squad?" Hoping that I already knew the answer to my question, I confidently slid my rook another space again blocking my king from danger.

"He has," Ollamh offered without taking his eyes off the chess board and adding, "I'm sure he'd rather tell you himself although he didn't tell me not to say anything." Again, sliding his bishop, Ollamh repeated, "Check" and before I could scan the board for my next move he added, "Mate!" The game was over for that moment. But, as I would soon find out, officially from King Edgar, a new game was about to begin.

Just then there was a knock at the door. Opening the door, I discovered Mitchell, a young squire that I knew well. Mitchell was apprenticed to King Edgar and spent most days in and around the Great Hall running errands and serving Edgar any way he could in the hopes of one day becoming a knight. Clearly winded, Mitchell said, "Sir Nathaniel, King Edgar asked me to fetch you to the Great Hall at once. His Majesty has a matter of great importance to discuss with you." I smiled at the formal announcement. Mitchell was a good boy and worked hard to carry out his duties efficiently and thoroughly. I thanked him for his message, slipped him a coin for his efforts, and followed his hurried steps to the Great Hall. As a trusted adviser to King Edgar, and my personal tutor, Ollamh enjoyed many freedoms in the castle. One such liberty was being party to private conversations. Naturally, as I trailed Mitchell to my meeting with the king, Ollamh shadowed me through the winding corridors and took his place in the Great Hall.

-5-

King Edgar was standing over a long wooden table leaning both hands on the boards and staring down at a detailed map of Westerford and the surrounding kingdoms. Without looking up the king said, "Nat, come look at this map and tell me what you see." I stepped forward and scanned the map for a minute or two before speaking. Staring at the map I noticed many natural borders: the mountain range to the north that included the highest peak, Mount Uasal; Tranglam Forest to the east; and, to the west, beyond Lake Machnamh, were Dragon Veil Falls and its sheer cliffs climbing high to a distant wasteland. Westerford seemed to be well protected by natural boundaries. Of course there was the dry riverbed, just west of Mount Uasal, which separated Westerford from Comharsa, her neighbor to the north. The one fringed by massive shrubbery that Danby and I had ignited the last time our kingdom was under attack – the very deed that led directly to my knighthood, quest, marriage to Charis, and future as King of Westerford. I knew too well that the dry riverbed appeared to be a weakness in our defenses.

The only other chink in our defenses would be the old road through Tranglam Forest. But, the map showed that road to be narrow and winding. Travelers spoke of terrifying sights and sounds in the forest. It was said that Tranglam Forest was haunted. And as such few would venture that direction. Certainly not enough troops to successfully attack a kingdom the size of Westerford.

After considering the map and every scenario I could think of, I spoke, "King Edgar, it seems to me that our kingdom is naturally fortified on most borders." Edgar nodded and waited for the "but."

"But," I continued, "The riverbed west of Uasal is still the weakest point of defense in my opinion. Also, and it would take a very brave enemy to attempt it, Tranglam Forest is virtually unprotected and would provide covered passage for any army willing to travel that old road. Of course an attack by sea from the south is always possible but the landing there is treacherous and there is nothing on that coast to attack. Troops would have to beach their ships and travel many miles by land to attack Westerford and infantry troops with that level of military expertise would not be the skilled sailors it would take to reach our shores and safely land their ships," I said at last. "No," I added, "Other than the riverbed between Westerford and Comharsa, and, of course, Tranglam Forest we are well-protected, Sire," I finished and looked to Ollamh who nodded his agreement with my assessment.

After a brief pause to consider, King Edgar said, "You are absolutely right, Nat," and turning to Ollamh he said, "You have taught him well Ollamh, thank you. Now what to do about it?" The king finished with an open question.

I cleared my throat to speak and Edgar waited patiently to hear what I had to say. "Your Majesty, if I may be so bold as to borrow your own wise idea," I began, "Allow me to select a small band of knights to create a specialized force trained to observe and track, trained to fight and live off the land. We could patrol the weaker borders watching for enemy activity and acting as a first line of defense and warning for the kingdom. With Danby at my side I could set up a system of signal fires to notify the rest of your knights in the event of attack."

The king stared at me thoughtfully for several seconds before responding. His face cracked into a broad smile behind that big beard of his and he laughed, "That, my boy, is exactly what we should do. Sir Nathaniel, you are hereby charged to select six other knights from my King's Guard. They will report directly to you and you will report directly to me. Your training should be rigorous in all the areas we discussed, including visiting the riverbed border to plan our defense of that area. Once you have selected your squad I will host a tournament of skill to test your knights to ensure they are truly qualified for such a dangerous and important mission."

-6-

In addition to training as a knight and tending to my education under Ollamh's watchful eye, Danby and I spent as much time together as we could. Awake with the sunrise, I would kiss Charis good morning and wish her a wonderful day doing whatever it was she did while I was away. She would give me a smile and tell me to have fun keeping the kingdom safe all the while knowing that I would be flying with Danby and spending the rest of my day training with the King's Guard or studying with Ollamh. I imagined that Charis spent her days doing things that a princess does. Besides being tutored in reading and writing, she likely would practice her embroidery, gossip with her ladies-in-waiting, and learn to oversee the castle staff. Charis would, after all, one day be Queen of Westerford.

-7-

It was easy to hop out of bed knowing that my daily routine began with soaring through the blue morning sky on Danby's back. It was my favorite duty, if you could truly call it a duty, each morning to fly high over the kingdom checking to see that all was well.

Knowing that we would be flying by, the villagers, waking up from their night's rest, would start their day by stepping outside to wave good morning to Danby the Dragon. Many villagers took time out of their day to stop by the training field or the castle on their way to market just to tell me how seeing Danby and I zoom overhead quickened their hearts and gave them a smile to start their day. Knowing that Danby was on duty provided a sense of safety that no army or militia could give. And, although the people still held a twinge of fear from years of stories about wicked dragons, everyone knew that they could count on Danby to defend them and keep them safe from trouble.

Our morning flights were not merely for fun, nor were they only to check on the kingdom and its inhabitants. Those daily flights were practice and exercise. There was no training manual to read when it came to riding a dragon. Trial and error was the basis of our training. Danby and I knew each other so well and trusted each other so completely that flying together was neither frightening nor dangerous. Oh, we had our share of near misses from time to time, but Danby was an amazing athlete and was able to physically control any situation.

On a few occasions, while working on low-level flying, we came dangerously close to hitting a tree or an outcrop of rock. One such flight always comes to mind when I think about near misses. It was early one spring morning and the smoke from the village mingled with the morning fog to create a blue-gray blanket over the forest. I directed Danby towards the forest low and fast. We could hardly see the trees until we were right among them. Danby rolled on his right side to squeeze through a narrow gap in the trees and, as he leveled out, a large flock of geese lifted from a small forest pond where they had rested for the night. As Danby and I shot into the clearing the geese beat the air with their wings, honking loudly seemingly to alarm the forest of their danger. Acting quickly, instead of turning nose-up, as would seem logical to avoid a collision while flying low, Danby dipped even lower toward the pond skimming his belly on the water. In an instant the geese were above us and moments later we rose safely back to a comfortable elevation.

-8-

Once our morning flight was complete and our aerial training finished for the day, we headed toward our meeting place where we would train with the King's Guard Knights. Danby and I would land near the training grounds just south of the castle where the King's Guard worked daily honing their skills. Some were out patrolling the kingdom, while others remained behind to train. By the time I arrived, many of the King's Guards were already deep into their work and I had to warm up quickly to catch up with the knights already on the pitch.

There was a cool meadow near the training grounds where Danby would spend his days relaxing in the sunshine, drinking from a cool spring that fed the small stream that crossed the meadow. Not far from the meadow was a small forest, a grove of trees really, where Danby found shade when the weather turned hotter. And, just inside the grove was a low stone barn with a thatched roof that blended into the landscape. It had a large opening and served as a shelter for Danby so that he was always nearby. King Edgar himself loved to visit Danby. He made sure that his little shelter was kept clean and that Danby was well fed. The king even brought Danby treats when he visited. He was a happy dragon.

-9-

As my training in every aspect of knighthood progressed under the tutelage of Ollamh, King Edgar checked on me regularly to see how things were going. He was pleased that I was a quick learner and had already given me my first assignment as the leader of the King's Guard and heir to the throne of Westerford.

King Edgar wanted me to select and develop a small band of top-notch knights to represent him throughout the kingdom. He had visions that this group of highly skilled warriors would complete dangerous missions in his name and take on other duties of importance to the king himself. I agreed that a team of knights like that would be valuable to King Edgar and was excited about the task set before me.

The king gave me free reign to select a crew of six other knights from the King's Guard. The seven of us would train together in all things "knightly" until we acted as one unit in the name of king and kingdom. What did I know about choosing knights? I had only been a knight for several months and, although my training had been rigorous, it was hardly complete.

-10-

I knew many of the knights from our work on the training grounds and I knew from my studies and own adventures what I would look for in a comrade.

My childhood friend, Chase, who I'd grown up with in Sutter, my home village, was an easy selection. He was loyal and true and, since we'd been friends for so very long, I was confident he would never lie to me or give me advice just because he thought it was what I wanted to hear. I could count on Chase to be honest with me, always. You might wonder how Chase, the blacksmith's son, came to be a knight. It seems that, traditionally, all attendants to the bride and groom in a royal wedding must be of noble rank. However, many years ago, when "Fat" King Bert was marrying the common, but beautiful, Veronica, an exception was made by royal decree so that Veronica's sisters, Carly and Nicole, could attend her as bridesmaids in the royal wedding party.

Since it was an official royal decree, both Carly and Nicole were made Ladies of the Royal Court in the eyes of the law. It was this same law, named the "Bridal Decree," that allowed me to select my friend, Chase, as "Best Man" for my wedding even though he was not a knight. As a result of the "Bridal Decree," King Edgar knighted Chase and declared him a member of the King's Guard alongside me.

-11-

Chase was an easy selection. But, there were five more knights to choose out of the 100 knights in the King's Guard. I had spent time with all of the King's Guard Knights during my few months in the castle. All sorts of training – swords, shields, pikes, and longbow, on foot and on horseback – gave me the chance to see all the knights at work. I quickly discovered that the best time to judge a knight was when he was not training. During down time or at meals was when a knight's true character showed.

It was easy to pick out strengths and weaknesses when working so closely with the other knights every day. It was obvious that all of the King's Guard Knights had great skills and "knightly" qualities. But, some of the knights just stood out as having something more than the others. A certain quality separated them from their peers. The other knights treated them with a different level of respect. This was not because of rank. It was clear this level of respect was earned based on intangible qualities.

There was one knight who stood out immediately. His name was Garrett and he was a little bit older than most of the others. He was taller than most, too. But, what made him a clear choice was his ability to see a situation or problem from many different sides and choose the best possible response to it. Garrett was strong and exceedingly smart. The other knights deferred to Garrett because they trusted his judgment. Garrett's skill with a sword was a clear bonus. But, it was also his ingenuity that drew me to him. He could visualize a problem before it occurred, formulate a plan for overcoming the obstacle and was skilled enough to construct apparatus needed to complete the task. Garrett, with his experience, more than many knights in the King's Guard, had traveled extensively around the kingdom. He was born of a noble family from the far end of Westerford and had been a member of the King's Guard since his father sent him to King Edgar as a squire on his 15th birthday.

Another knight who stood out among his peers was Kevin. Built like a mountain, Kevin was, by far, the strongest of the King's Guard Knights. A natural leader, Kevin was the hardest worker of all the knights in Edgar's service. Given a task to complete, Kevin would not rest until it was done. Somewhat stubborn, he would not accept failure. Skilled with sword and shield, Kevin wielded an enormous battle-ax that would take most men two hands to lift and every bit of strength to swing. He could hold his iron rimmed shield in one hand and swing that ax with the other laying waste to enemy warriors with every stroke. In addition to Kevin's skill in battle, the other knights looked up to him for his perseverance and undying tenacity. Kevin was from the hill country in the farthest northern part of Westerford. He kept his blond hair long, but tied it back with a leather cord except during battle when he let it fly wildly about his head. Though he was cool in battle, Kevin believed his untamed locks struck fear into his opponents who thought him to be just as wild as his hair.

One of the youngest knights was Christopher. Possessed of incredible intelligence and logic, "Chris" was never swayed by emotion. He made decisions based on intellect and reason. Chris was also very athletic. Not as big as Garrett, nor as strong as Kevin, Chris would not back down in the face of danger. He would plan his attacks, evaluate his opponent's weaknesses and, with the quickest of strokes, disarm his foe leaving him begging for mercy. Choosing not to carry an unbalanced shield, Chris used his quickness and intelligence. With blinding speed Chris wielded a sword in one hand, for hacking and chopping, and a seax, or short sword, in his other hand for quick thrusts and slashing. Born on the shores of Lake Machnamh, Chris was at home both on the water and in it.

My fifth selection took some serious thought. There were so many knights to choose from, and all had their own special qualities. As I looked around the training yard one particular knight caught my eye. His focus and accuracy with the longbow was truly amazing. The archery field was set up with multiple targets both stationary and moving – some swinging, some rolling, all very challenging. Ryan was the knight's name and he didn't miss. But, what impressed me as much as Ryan's accuracy was the joy with which he engaged his training. Laughing and joking with the other knights, Ryan truly loved what he was doing. He had an infectious personality, entertaining his peers while he worked so that the work became joy and the day's toil melted into a pleasure that resembled children at play. Ryan was having fun, and my company could use some fun. He was from a large cattle ranch near the foothills of Mount Uasal. Born of a wealthy ranch family, Ryan was comfortable with animals big and small. He was especially skilled at carving the best meat from the hunt and preparing it for eating. His many abilities would come in handy to my team while we traveled the countryside.

With one exception, I had decided which knights I wanted on my team. All trained knights with skill, intelligence, leadership, bravery and personality. With an element of youth on our side, this crew would become the core of the King's Guard Knights for many years to come.

But, King Edgar had instructed me to select a team of six knights. Their skills should complement each other and they should be knights of strong character. The belief in living a "knightly" life must show clearly in everything they did, every decision they made and every reason they chose for drawing their weapons. Although my squad needed King Edgar's blessing I knew these knights were the ones I wanted to ride with into battle in the name of Westerford.

-12-

One knight, while on the training field, made a different kind of impression on me. His work was unlike the others. Not quite as tall as many of the knights, he had a lean and athletic build. His shining, silver armor and plain white shield were finely made but showed no family crest or other defining marks except for a painted red fox running across the center of his shield. The only other distinguishable marking was that his helmet was forged with the long ears and snout of a fox. He was not exceptionally strong. But, made up for his lack of power with quickness and skill that rivaled the best knights of the King's Guard. A curious fellow, he never spoke and never removed his helmet. He was all business and once his training was finished, he mounted his horse and rode away only to return for the next day's training session, bright and early, always already on the training pitch by the time I arrived from working with Danby.

I had chosen the other knights for my squad based on leadership skills, strength, speed, personality, and their interactions with other knights. However, it was his unassuming nature and desire to go unnoticed that intrigued me. Perhaps this mystery knight was the one my team needed to make it complete. His skill and swiftness perfectly complimented the strength and power of my other knights. He was the missing piece.

I spoke to Ollamh about this mysterious knight and he agreed that the skill and speed would create balance. Ollamh also noted that the knight was exceptionally intelligent as well, with common sense and intuition unrivaled by any knight he had met. I asked Ollamh to give me his name so that I could recruit him to join my team. All that Ollamh said was, "That information belongs to King Edgar himself to share."

Very well, I thought to myself, I would make one more attempt to speak to this mystery knight on my own and if he continued to elude me I would have to find some other way. Since Edgar was making his annual trek throughout the kingdom to visit all of the villages, I would have to wait until the week before the King's Tournament to ask his permission for this knight to join us. My team, incomplete though it was, would have to train without our sixth knight until I could ask Edgar myself.

-13-

My attempts to befriend the "mystery" knight came up empty as he seemed to ignore my efforts at conversation. I made up my mind that it wasn't just me that he eluded. He seemed to keep everyone at arm's length during training, but his businesslike work habits drew me to him all the more. Most of his interactions came by way of hand signals and gestures with an occasional "yes" or "no" answer muffled through the faceguard of his helmet. I was determined that he should join my group and approached him about it one day as we sparred with swords and shields.

He was quick but I was stronger. He was far more skilled as a swordsman than I was as demonstrated during a training match we shared. We exchanged an especially heated series of blows that resulted in me backing away until I ended up flat on my back with the mystery knight's sword point aimed dangerously close to my throat. We were as close as we had ever been so, while I was already at a disadvantage, I seized my opportunity and said, "Sir Knight, I would like to know your name and ask, with respect, that you join with me as I form an elite band of warriors in the name of King Edgar." Without a word the knight withdrew his sword from my throat, offered me his hand and, once I was back on my feet, turned away, quickly mounting his horse that stood nearby. Before spurring his horse he turned and shouted in a voice muffled by his helmet, "I would, but it's not my choice." With that one sentence I knew my team would be complete if I could get the king's permission for the mystery knight to join us.

I shook my head and smiled, brushed the dust from the back of my armor and ran to find Danby where he was relaxing in the meadow. I jumped on his back and in a flash we were airborne. I didn't want the mystery knight to know I was following him so I leaned back so that Danby would climb up, up, up above the wispy clouds just so I could see which direction the knight was riding. Imagine my surprise when I saw him ride straight across the old wooden drawbridge into Westerford Castle!

Without officially receiving an answer from the "mystery" knight I made plans for him to join our crew as soon as I was able to speak to King Edgar and receive his permission. It seemed odd to me that I couldn't just approach the knight on my own. But, as I learned almost daily there was a lot more to running a kingdom than most people knew. And, it was rarely easy.

-14-

With the King's Tournament approaching in only a month, I met with each of the knights I had chosen to join me. King Edgar set up his tournament as a final test of skill for all of his knights before I could make my team official. Each knight knew that my opinion was valued, but King Edgar would have the final say as to which knights would represent him and the kingdom. With that understanding in mind, each of the knights eagerly accepted the challenge before him.

We set out to become the best. We trained day and night honing our skills with sword and shield, bow and arrow; any number of weapons at our disposal became deadly in our hands. We also worked on our navigational skills learning to find our way by following the sun or reading the evening stars. My comrades and I could track and hunt game, and we could build fire and shelter out of the barest materials to keep warm and dry when the weather turned sour. Of course the fire-starting skill was rarely necessary since we were never far from Danby.

My team of knights would be the best combination of skill, strength, speed and intelligence. We would train together until we became one unit – working together for king and kingdom.

-15-

Training as a group was difficult at the King's Guard training fields since all of the knights interacted with one another equally throughout the day. So, I decided it was time we tested our skills in a different location. I told the five other knights to pack enough gear for one week, that we were taking a trip.

The next morning we met, as planned, at sunrise in the grove near the training ground. Our horses stamped the soft turf and chomped at their bits nervously anticipating what might come next. The knights, on the other hand, were calm and ready just as well-trained soldiers should be. Although they didn't know what to expect, they were prepared for anything.

I had decided that it was time to return to the dry riverbed that marked the northern border of Westerford and separated our kingdom from Comharsa, the kingdom to our immediate north. It would be a reconnaissance trip of sorts. I wanted to see what kind of defense the riverbed truly provided. We would mark weak areas on our maps and plan out what sort of defensive walls or barriers could be built in those weak places. Finally, I would make a few high elevation passes across the border with Danby to see, first-hand, what kind of troop build-up was actually taking place. These activities would all be part of my team's normal mission. We would not engage the enemy unless absolutely necessary. We were only traveling to train and observe.

The weather was perfect for our trip and we rode through the countryside stopping at villages along the way always heading north. Six knights riding together raised no suspicions even though we were armored and carrying fully stocked saddlebags and bedrolls for overnight. We did, however, draw some attention because we were never far from the shadow of a dragon. Every villager knew of Danby so they also safely assumed that I was among the troop traveling through their village.

Each day along the way we stopped to train as we always did, with sword and shield or bow and arrow. The best part about those first few days was that there was plenty of time for us to get to know each other. These knights were men I quickly came to love and admire as friends and brothers. I felt deep in my heart that my choices had been right and true. They were men I would charge into battle with and defend to the death. But, most importantly, they would be excellent ambassadors for Westerford and represent the king and kingdom with honor and respect.

-16-

On the third day of our trek, we reached the southern bluff of the dry riverbed. We could see Comharsa from where we camped overlooking the ravine. I was happy to see that the brush that created an additional natural barrier had grown back more thick and full than it was before Danby and I burned it so many years before. Danby seemed to remember that night we lit the brush alerting the King's Guard to help defend Westerford from attack. I remembered that night as the beginning of my good fortune.

While my comrades set up camp for the night, I climbed onto Danby's shoulders and with a great flap of his powerful wings we were soon soaring high over the northern Westerford countryside. It was a lovely evening to fly but I needed to focus on my task. I had to see where our kingdom was vulnerable to attack and come up with a plan to reinforce our northern border. We flew low along the southern edge of the dry riverbed. At one time the river was wide and deep, but now, even during a wet year, the river was little more than a lazy creek meandering its way toward the sea between two tall bluffs. The width of the river I estimated based on the distance between the bluffs had to be at least a mile or more. It would have made a formidable natural barrier for our kingdom. Now the distance would barely slow a well-planned attack.

Leaning back Danby turned his nose toward the darkening sky up into the chill air high above the countryside. When we were high enough to appear as no more than a high-flying bird, we turned north to see what the Comharsana were up to. It didn't take long to see that there was some sort of activity below. Fires burned brightly in the villages as the people settled in for the night. One area in particular caught my eye. A couple of miles north of the riverbed appeared to be a fortified city. It was protected from view by a dense forest that stood between the fortress and our border. This was no small country village but a large city surrounded by a wood and dirt rampart designed to keep invaders out. They were preparing for some sort of conflict and King Edgar would want to know details. From Danby's back high among the clouds I could only see shapes and make guesses at what was actually going on below. To get any real information for the king we would need to get closer. Without a word I nudged Danby gently and he made a long sweeping turn back to camp.

Around the fire that night I explained to the knights what I had seen. They agreed that the king would want to know as much information as we could discover about Comharsa. We had to cross the border and take a closer look.

-17-

The air was cool and damp when I awoke the next morning long before the sun broke the eastern horizon. Our trek that day would be only a few miles. But, those few miles would be dangerous and difficult. There were not wide, clearly marked paths in this part of Westerford and I knew it would be slow going on the other side of the border. The dry riverbed was wide open and we would have to be on the other side before day broke to avoid detection. I honestly wasn't sure what awaited us across the riverbed. All I knew was that we were crossing open borderland and entering Comharsa, a neighboring, potentially hostile, kingdom.

Although we were not planning any sort of aggressive action, just being discovered within the Comharsana borders could be considered an act of war. We knew we had to be careful not to be caught. Our months of training would truly be tested.

We ate our breakfast of hard bread and dried meat without building a fire and without much conversation. Securing our horses to the trees around our campsite, we made our final preparations for our short, but treacherous journey. When we were ready to go I called to Danby. He seemed to know something important was going on. I could tell by the look in his eyes, or maybe he could tell by the look in mine. While I ran my hand along his neck, I whispered into his ear, "Danby, we need to explore the fortified city to see what the Comharsana are up to." Danby nodded and stamped his foot letting me know that he understood. "I want you to fly high up among the clouds where even we can't see you to watch over us and make sure we are safe until we get into that forest. Once we are under cover of the forest, I want you to return here and protect our horses and wait for our return." Without a sound Danby nodded and, with a great flap of his wings, he was airborne. I craned my neck and watched as he flew higher and higher until he was no more than a speck in the early morning sky.

With Danby soaring above for support, we wasted no time beginning our mission. Crawling single file through the brush was perhaps going to be the most difficult part of the mission. While Danby and I had been exploring the area by air, Kevin and Chris had taken it upon themselves to survey the natural barrier along the edge of the riverbed. During their exploration they had noticed that there were gaps midway between the trunks where the extending branches of the shrubs intermingled to create the full barrier. We had to lie down and crawl through the opening on our bellies one after another. I led the way and discovered as soon as I pushed my way out the other side of the bush that the barrier truly was growing right on the edge of the bluff. I tumbled headlong down the steep hill and landed with a thump in a pile of deep sand at the edge of the dry riverbed. The landing was soft and caused no pain, at least not until my five companions landed on top of me one after the other. If not for the serious nature of our mission, we all would have laughed out loud. We saved our merriment for another day, dusted ourselves off and prepared to make our way across the riverbed as quickly as we could.

-18-

We knew crossing the dry riverbed would be dangerous. Until we arrived safely on the other side, we would be completely exposed, with no cover at all, to whomever might be standing on the bluffs on either side. Deciding that it would be better to spread out than to run across the sand in a large group, we separated, leaving a gap of about 40 feet between us. I glanced into the sky as if checking that Danby was looking out for us, and then I signaled the others with a wave of my hand. Driven by excitement and the fear of getting caught, we ran low and fast. We covered the distance between the bluffs in a matter of a few minutes finally regrouping on the other side. We found cover under a large oak tree that we had seen growing precariously on the northern bluff as if hanging on to the opposite wall for fear of falling into what was once a raging river.

Catching our breath in the shadow of the mighty oak we sipped some water from the skins that we carried in our packs and nibbled on a bit of dry bread to keep up our energy. The next part of our journey would be the most dangerous. The morning sky was just beginning to change color as the sun finally broke the eastern horizon. We had to take care to avoid the villages and decided to stay in the forest for cover. The Comharsana would be waking to begin their day. Seeing a troop of warriors from Westerford would certainly raise the alarm.

So far I had felt fairly safe knowing that Danby was watching from somewhere high above. However, entering the darkness and shadows of the forest filled me with a sudden fear that my warriors and I had crossed into a hostile kingdom without direct permission from King Edgar. This could be considered an act of war even though our intention was only to gather information. I steeled my thoughts and continued on through the darkness of the forest.

Had we been safely back in Westerford, I would have found the forest quite lovely and the going easy. But, since we had to be wary of every noise and shadow, the forest passage was anything but pleasant. Suddenly, I heard the sharp crack of a breaking twig followed by a loud whooshing sound as wind rushing through the trees. I turned toward the sounds and heard shouting from Kevin, Ryan, and Chase. They had tripped a booby trap and were swooped into the trees by a large cargo net. Garrett, Chris, and I swiftly drew our weapons and stood back to back beneath our comrades looking for an enemy. But, none came forward.

The shadowy forest darkness played tricks on my eyes. I was imagining enemies in every breeze blowing through the branches and every shadow on the forest floor. I stepped back, turning slowly, searching the darkness when I lost my balance and fell head over heels into a pit twice as deep as I was tall. The sides of the pit were straight and smooth so climbing out would be impossible.

Garrett and Chris rushed to my aid and tripped another trap that sent them both into the trees suspended from a rope by their ankles upside-down. We were trapped. As I began to consider my options, I heard laughter coming from somewhere deep among the trees. I shouted and my knights shouted, but all we heard was laughter.

-19-

"Show yourself!" I demanded. Although trapped as we were I wasn't sure I was in any position to make demands. Just then the laughter turned to the most pleasant music I had ever heard. The voice was sweet and the melody soothing. My eyelids grew very heavy and before I could say another word I was dreaming peaceful dreams with the words repeating themselves in my head:

Guests you are within my arms,
These woods are full of magic charms.

It's time to sleep not time to fight,
With darkness comes the morning light.

You've wandered into dangerous lands,
And fallen right into my hands.

A good thing too, now rest your head,
Another day you'd end up dead.

I'll help you find your way back home,
Next time, think before you roam.

I'll tell you all you need to know,
But then it's time for you to go.

I awoke with a start. I couldn't feel my hands. They were tied tightly at the wrists behind my back. I looked around, my eyes still heavy with sleep. I could see my companions, all tied as I was and all waking up and clearing their heads too. We sat on the floor in the corner of a very strange room.

Looking around I realized that the room was very small indeed. The ceiling was low with dark wooden beams crisscrossing from wall to wall and what seemed to be roots interwoven between them. Similar dark beams, wound about with roots that seemed to grow right down into the floor, were standing at intervals around the room apparently supporting the low ceiling. The walls seemed to be constructed of dirt but they were so smooth and straight it was hard to tell for sure – I was still a little groggy from my nap. As the fog of sleep lifted from my head I could tell that we were in a sort of cave. But, it wasn't like any of the dirty caves that I had experienced in my life. This cave was more like a comfortable little house. The floor was neatly swept and there were small, colorful rugs scattered here and there. A brightly decorated cupboard constructed of wood stood from floor to ceiling in one corner and along one wall there was a small table with two small chairs built from the branches of what appeared to be a beech tree..

Built right into another side wall was a bright, friendly fireplace burning warmly. Bathed in the fire's golden glow were overstuffed armchairs with high backs. Seated comfortably in one of the armchairs with his legs crossed at the ankles on the stone hearth was the strangest looking little man. He had bright red hair that stuck out at all angles from his head. He had a matching red beard and was dressed from head to toe in a suit of deep forest green. No wonder we couldn't see him, I thought, he perfectly matched the colors and shadows of the forest. His cheeks were red from the fire and his eyes twinkled with a happy gleam. Without saying a word, the little man sat there in his little chair close to the fireplace just looking at my friends and me and puffing on a long-stemmed pipe.

Just as I opened my mouth to speak, a door swung open and a small woman backed into the room carrying a small wooden tray loaded with treats. She was plump and looked just like the little man, without the beard. She wore a dress of the same deep forest green color worn by the little man. Looking at me from across the room she set the tray on the small wooden table and smiled a welcoming smile.

"Good morning, Nat," she said as if she had said it every morning of her life.

Confused, but not wanting to be rude, I said, "Good morning, and how do you know my name?"

The little man and woman laughed the very same happy laughter that I had heard in the woods. Rising from his chair by the fire, the man said, "There are many voices in the forests of the world and they have many stories to tell. You would be wise to listen to the voices and befriend them."

I nodded, bewildered, and looked at my mates who were equally as baffled as I at our strange predicament. Though they obviously decided it best to keep quiet and allow me to do the talking.

"My name is Brainse, and this is my wife, Duille. We have lived here in the forest for many years. It is our chosen duty to care for the forest and all who live here." Brainse said in a friendly, singsong voice.

"Please accept my most humble apologies, Brainse, for my friends and me trespassing in your forest." I began, but was interrupted by another great burst of that familiar, happy laughter.

"It is not our forest. The forest belongs to no one and to everyone. We are only here to care for it and keep it safe."

Drawing a knife that was sheathed at his side Brainse walked slowly toward me, still smiling as he came. I tried to back away but was pressed against the wall when Brainse began again, "You are too suspicious, Nat. Fear not, I do not intend any more harm to you than you intend to the forest. I am trying to cut your bonds so that we can share a meal and some friendly conversation, then you and your friends may be on your way."

I breathed a great sigh of relief and turned so that Brainse could cut the rope. Rubbing my numb wrists, the feeling began returning to my hands, first with tingling then with a dull ache until they finally felt normal again. I could see from the other knights that their hands felt the same way. From their expression I could tell that they were as happy as I was to be loose.

Standing to my full height I nearly bumped my head on the ceiling and, although I knew they were small, I realized just how tiny Brainse and Duille actually were. They barely came up to my waist when they stood at their full height. Yet, they had captured six knights without drawing a weapon. Truly there was a strong magic at work here in this forest.

"In my dream I heard a voice singing sweetly," I began again.

"That was my voice singing you and your companions to sleep. I could hardly get you all into my home otherwise," replied Brainse kindly.

"Where are we?" I asked.

"You are in our home among the roots of the forest. Notice how the twisting roots of the great trees decorate our humble home," he answered pointing to the interwoven roots zigzagging their way over the ceiling and down the support beams of the tiny room.

Duille added, "It is good that we came along when we did. Comharsan soldiers are searching the forest as we speak for a troop of invaders from the south."

"We only came to see the fortified city on the other side of the forest. I fear that Comharsa is planning an attack on Westerford," I said softly, trying not to sound too anxious. I added, "Your song said that you would tell me all I need to know. What can you tell me about that fortress? Does the king of Comharsa plan to invade Westerford?" I asked with genuine concern in my voice.

My friends and I sat on the floor of the tiny room while Duille passed around her wooden tray of delicious snacks. Brainse poured a bright green liquid into tiny wooden cups and passed a cup to each of us. The drinks were every bit as tasty and refreshing as Duille's snacks. Once we had all been served Brainse and Duille settled into their seats by the fire and, lighting his long pipe, Brainse began to speak again.

"It is true there is a new city in Comharsa built within a few short miles of the Westerford border. There are more than one hundred trained warriors living within the fortress and they oversee the villages that surround their walls." I leaned forward expecting more and Brainse didn't disappoint.

"Within the city, among his warriors, dwells a warlord named Achrann. He does not currently set his sights on Westerford, although his fortress is treacherously close to her borders. Achrann is preparing for civil war within Comharsa," Brainse said as a tear spilled from his eye and rolled down his cheek. His deep sadness touched my heart.

"What can we do to help your plight?" I asked knowing that it was not truly my fight.

At this Duille spoke up, "It is kind of you to offer, Nat. But, at this time there is nothing you can do. Your future in Westerford takes a long and winding path. One that will intertwine with many kingdoms before its end. Do not forget our small kindness, Nat. One day Comharsa will need you and you will return to repay our bit of kindness many times over."

I felt a strange sensation that Duille spoke truth and I bowed my head to them both as I vowed to remember them and their gentle ways.

"If ever it is within my power to aid you and your Comharsana during a time of need, I pledge to do all that I can to repay your kindness."

"Thank you, Nat. You will be a valued ally in the future when the paths of our kingdoms shall cross again," said Brainse. "But, for now, you must return to Westerford. You have much to do before you can help the Comharsana. At this time Achrann and his warriors are searching the forest. You must be on your way."

With obvious concern in my voice I asked, "How will we return to Westerford with warriors searching the forest?"

Smiling broadly, Brainse arose from his soft chair by the fire, and opened a door in the wall that none of us had noticed until then.

"Follow these stairs down until, at the bottom, you reach a long tunnel. The tunnel is not well-lit, but it is smooth and straight so there is no danger of tripping or running into obstacles. The tunnel will lead you to another stairway – one that climbs. At the top of that stair is a door that will open onto the meadow where you left your ponies," Brainse instructed with a magical twinkle in his eye.

Standing as one, trying not to bump our heads on the ceiling, my knights and I bowed and thanked Brainse and Duille for their hospitality and information.

"But," I began to formulate another question. Brainse held up his hand and said, "Trust us in all we have said and return the kindness when you are in position to do so. You will be a great leader. You have already chosen wisely. Continue to seek the mystery knight. Oh, and your friend awaits you in the meadow." Brainse said with a wink.

With that we turned and hurried through the secret doorway. We raced through the tunnel until we found the stairs at the other end. At the top of the stairs was a door, just as Brainse had said there would be. Turning the knob, I gave a gentle push and there we were, magically returned to our campsite, our horses, and, of course, my friend, Danby, right where I had told him to wait for us.

It was twilight so we built a fire and cooked our evening meal. Discussing our adventure quietly we agreed that the king would definitely want to know everything.

-20-

We spent the next day riding along the border and planning basic fortification. There was plenty of natural stone that could be used to build a low wall just behind the natural brush barrier. An enemy climbing the high bluff and passing through dense brush only to be met with a stone wall would make any sort of real attack very difficult. On the following day, with a plan firmly in our minds, we packed up and rode back toward the castle to report our findings to the king.

On our way home we were traveling through the woods near Sutter, the village where Chase and I grew up, when I had a great idea. Chase's father was the village blacksmith. Chase's father was called "Blackie," though no one actually knew his given name. His face was dark from the smoke and flames of the forge and he was well muscled from many years of swinging heavy hammers and molding steel into bright blades and armor. Blackie was well known throughout the kingdom for his skill and expertise with metal. He was much more than just the man to see when your horse threw a shoe – Blackie was a true artist.

When we were young, visiting Blackie was always fun and that warm afternoon was no different. As we approached Blackie's forge, the anvil sang as the hammers clanged shaping steel and iron. I asked Blackie if he would make custom armor for my team. He said that he would and took our measurements to help complete the job. He told us to return in one month, on the next full moon, to retrieve our new armor.

In the meantime, we continued training harder than ever knowing that having custom armor might prove premature if the outcome of the King's Tournament was not what I hoped.

However, I was confident my knights would demonstrate to King Edgar the skills that drew my attention to them in the first place.

With only one month until the King's Tournament I knew what I had to do. As soon as we returned home I would meet with King Edgar to discuss the mystery knight. I slept soundly in my comfortable bed and, as always, awoke with the sunrise, kissed Charis good morning, and joined Danby for our morning flight. It was glorious.

-21-

Knowing that I still needed one more knight to complete my outfit weighed heavily on my mind so it was time to see the king to discover the identity of the mystery knight. The next day, after my morning flight with Danby, I went to the castle and asked Gregory, King Edgar's steward, for a brief meeting with the king. While I waited in the Great Hall for Edgar's response, I looked around at the giant tapestries on the wall as I had done on every visit since I was a child. I loved those tapestries; their lively colors and the tales they depicted made my imagination run wild. It seemed every visit to the Great Hall yielded some new picture that I had never noticed before. This particular trip was no different. On one tapestry, high up on the wall, I noticed a forest scene in the background of a picture. In the foreground was a handsome young knight on a giant white horse. I thought, at first, that the knight was one of the kings from the past. But, all the other kings depicted on the tapestries had some sort of crown on their heads whether a real crown, a simple gold band, or even a wreath, there was always a crown of some sort. This knight had no crown so I assumed he was just a knight. I wondered about his story.

As impressive as it was, the knight in this particular tapestry did not seem to be the focal point of the piece. My eyes were drawn to the image of a lady, in flowing robes, dancing among an ancient stone circle. Her auburn hair seemed to wave, as though blown by the wind, although the tapestry itself hung perfectly still on the chamber wall. As I gazed at the tapestry, I felt a sadness that the knight seemed to be staring toward the lady of the forest with a look of anguish in his eyes like none I had ever seen before. I wondered who these characters were and what part of Westerford history they represented. My thoughts were suddenly shattered by a booming, boisterous voice I recognized in an instant. There was never any mistaking King Edgar's voice as he made his entrance into a room.

-22-

"Sir Nathaniel," the king exploded as he made his way into the Great Hall, "to what do we owe the pleasure of this surprise meeting?"

"Your Majesty," I began, bowing low to demonstrate my love and respect for Edgar.

"I've come to ask you for some information that, I'm told, only you have the power to give. And, my Lord, I believe you will be impressed with our training and some valuable information we have to share with you."

"My boy," smiled the king, "there is very little that I would not share with you. What is it that you'd like to know?"

With that response, I began my request, "As you have instructed, I have begun selecting my elite team of knights out of those already in training as members of the King's Guard." King Edgar smiled and nodded his understanding as I continued, "I believe I have discovered five of the finest knights we have. They eagerly have agreed to take part in Your Majesty's tournament with the goal of earning the right to join my squad and, in your honor, carry out duties throughout the kingdom. However, there is one knight who trains among us that I would like to add to the team. Although not the largest in stature or most powerful among the knights, he is swift of foot and has skills to rival our greatest swordsmen. He has obviously been training for many years with brilliant teachers."

With this, King Edgar interrupted, "If you've found a knight worthy of your team you have my blessing to invite him to join in the competition and, if he is truly worthy, make him part of that team. I'm not sure what my additional blessing has to do with it. I've already tasked you with creating a team of elite knights and given you permission to choose any knights you deem worthy from the knights in training with the King's Guard. You have my direction and full support in this matter. Invite him to the tournament."

"My Lord, I don't know the knight's name, nor can I discover his identity. He has many attributes that would be of value to my force including his obvious skill in the art of secrecy and stealth. As his helmet and shield would suggest he is truly as sly as a fox. He is the first knight on the pitch every day and the last to leave, never removing his helmet. I have spoken to him only once and he said that he would like to join my team but that it was not his choice." I assured the king that I had made every effort short of taking him down and wrestling his helmet from his head. I had even gone so far as to follow him as he left the training grounds only to discover that he rode right to Westerford Castle. I felt like I was complaining as I told Edgar my woes.

With that King Edgar placed his hand gently on my shoulder and assured me that he would discover the knight in question and allow him to choose whether he would like to compete to become part of my elite unit.

I thanked Edgar, bowing deeply again, and said, "One more thing, Lord, if you discover this knight and he chooses to join me, please send him to the blacksmith in the village of Sutter where I was raised. 'Blackie' is his name and there the knight will be fitted for a suit of armor to match the rest of my team. We are scheduled to pick up our new armor in one month's time, on the next full moon. Thank you, again, Your Majesty," I said as I turned to make my exit.

Before passing under the great stone archway and out through the heavy oaken doors, I took one last glance at the tapestry depicting the sad knight gazing back at the red haired lady dancing among the standing stones in the forest. I shivered with a sudden chill that, for reasons yet unknown to me, I would one day visit those standing stones.

-23-

The morning dew glistened on the tournament lawn like diamonds strewn across a green blanket. Pennants snapped in the crisp breeze and horses stamped their hooves in anticipation of the contest. King Edgar had called together all the knights of Westerford for a friendly competition of arms.

Although I had already selected my knights, I knew that checking their skills against others was a good idea to see if my assessment of their ability as warriors was accurate. I was certain that King Edgar would agree that these knights would represent Westerford well.

A stiff breeze whipped through the multi-colored tents that lined the tournament grounds. Inside the tents knights readied themselves for battle. True, the coming "battle" was only a controlled exercise in skill and merely an opportunity to demonstrate those skills before the King. It was important for each knight involved to show what they were capable of both for themselves and others in case they were ever called upon to defend the kingdom against a real enemy. No one was going to die today unless it was by horrible accident. Certainly, there could be injuries during the tournament. However, the knights would battle as if the kingdom was at stake and their life and the lives of their comrades depended on them.

The rules were simple: no stabbing with the point of the sword; that rule included knives, daggers, saexes, and any other apparatus with a point. No using the edge of a shield as a weapon, as shields, in this competition, were for blocking and unbalancing opponents only. In addition, combatants may only use the flat of the blade when striking an opponent in the head. No blows to the head with the edge of a blade. A blow to the head with the edge of a blade would result in immediate disqualification from the tournament. Finally, no bows and arrows – while this would likely hinder Ryan's chances of winning, I already knew that I needed an archer on my team and Ryan was that archer no matter how he did in this test of skill. In my mind I was curious to see what other skills Ryan might possess.

Everyone else that I had chosen for my team was there and readying themselves for battle. True, this competition was not "real" battle, but it was as close as we could get. It would be much more realistic than our daily training and King Edgar had already announced that he would personally present the best knights with rewards worthy of their prowess today.

-24-

Suddenly, my thoughts were interrupted by the sound of trumpets blaring a fanfare loud enough to wake the dead. The noise startled a flock of starlings that took wing from a nearby tree. The frightened birds circling the tents and tournament field added a brief, albeit panicked, aerial show to the colorful festivities.

King Edgar arose from his seat in the grandstand and, in his deep, booming voice, announced, "Ladies and gentlemen! Honored guests and esteemed combatants, please direct your attention to the west end of the tournament field."

Every head turned and a deafening cheer shattered an otherwise peaceful gathering as Danby approached low and fast, skimming the treetops at the west end of the pitch. He banked sharply over the grandstand, rolling first to his right side, then onto his back, and continuing again to his left side, before progressing once more so that he was right side up again. The crowd roared their approval and every head turned skyward as Danby gave one great flap of his powerful wings and accelerated straight up toward the heavens until he was nothing more than a dark green speck that disappeared into the blue morning sky.

Without warning the wind shifted again as Danby flew over the crowd from behind the grandstand, terrifying the audience for a moment with the speed and power with which he appeared out of nowhere. The instant burst of fear was quickly replaced with applause and screams of delight from the smiling faces.

Directly across the tournament field from the grandstand was what appeared to be a small army, made entirely of straw, standing at attention, battle-ready. I had assumed they had something to do with the tournament. I soon discovered that I was wrong. Danby, having already thrilled the crowd with his aerial skill, banked hard to his right to make one more pass over the pitch. At full speed he flew in close to the straw soldiers and, with a great burst from his lungs, Danby delighted the mesmerized crowd with a fire show that at once burned up the army of hay, brightening the cheering crowd with a dazzling orange glow. With a final pass and a great flap of his wings the windstorm that Danby created immediately blew out the flames.

With that, Danby's display of his skill in battle was over and the tournament was ready to begin. It suddenly became clear to me that King Edgar did more than give Danby treats while visiting him near the training grounds. This display must have been cooked up between the two of them while I was working on my own fighting skills.

-25-

There were approximately 100 knights armored and ready to begin. With blades and armor polished to a brilliant shine and shields painted with bright colors and the crest or symbol of each knights' family, the combatants lined the field facing King Edgar.

In his great, thundering voice Edgar addressed his knights. "Today is a marvelous day for the Kingdom of Westerford. The greatest young knights in the kingdom are assembled to compete in a 'friendly' display of skill-at-arms. We all know that this competition is not intended to demonstrate one's ability to chop and hack an opponent to death, but to show one's skill and speed, intelligence and strength."

A roar erupted from the crowded grandstand and King Edgar waited until it died down to continue. "This will be a 'Battle Royale' – every man for himself. The last man standing when the sun sets below the forest trees will be awarded the 'Champion's Medal' and 20 gold pieces!"

Another general roar from the crowd forced King Edgar to pause, a great smile creased his face and knights waved to the crowd, beat their shields with their swords and roared right back. They were excited and ready to begin.

"Finally," continued the king, "Sir Nathaniel and I will be watching carefully and making notes during the contest. We are forming an elite group of knights to become the lead unit in my 'King's Guard.' This team of knights will be leaders among my knights, they will engage in specialized training, and they will represent Westerford on select missions of a more complex nature. They will continue in my service, as will all of you gathered here, to be regarded as examples of what is good and right true throughout the kingdom. For all of you are the best and brightest in all of Westerford."

A third general roar erupted from the anxious crowd and King Edgar waited a third time for the noise to die down. "Noble Knights of Westerford!" He shouted in his deep voice that echoed throughout the countryside, "May the battle begin!" A flourish of trumpets sounded across the kingdom and the knights, lined up around the emerald field advanced as one, arms raised against their brothers in mock battle.

Sitting in the grandstand next to King Edgar with my lovely wife, Charis, seated on the other side of the king, and knowing, clearly, that this was merely a demonstration of skill, I still took no pleasure watching my brothers-in-arms attacking each other, for sport or not. From where I sat the tournament field had the odd appearance of a swarm of ants on an anthill. The rapid comings and goings around an ant colony looks out of control at first glance. However, a closer look revealed an organization and order to the seeming chaos.

-26-

As I sat with King Edgar watching the melee, I began scanning the field for the six knights I had already chosen. I wanted to see how they were faring in the battle.

Chase was easy to find. I had located him before the battle started. He looked big and powerful in his brightly shining armor. I had spent some time visiting with him in his tent the night before. The whole time we were talking, Chase was polishing his armor until he could see his reflection in the metallic surface. Chase's bright yellow shield with the black horse prancing in the center leaned against his armor rack in the corner of his tent. On the tournament field Chase's armor reflected the bright morning sunlight and his easily recognized shield let me know he was holding his own in the thick of the battle.

While I focused on Chase I saw him block a dangerous blow from a knight in dull gray armor who carried a red shield with a black cross painted on it. Chase immediately followed his block with a quick step to the side and a sword strike across the knight's back knocking him to the ground and, with that one blow, out of the fight.

It seemed knights were falling right and left, knocked out of the contest by fellow knights from King Edgar's court. Disappointment crossed each fallen knight's face, in turn followed rapidly by a shake of the head and a knowing smile. The smiles stemmed from the obvious realization that, although they were out of the competition, they were bested by a comrade, a teammate, a fellow knight, who someday might fight at his side in the face of a real enemy force.

As the mock battle raged, the sounds of metal clashing on metal and iron-rimmed shields blocking powerful sword strokes and ax blows rang across the pitch. The violent noise echoed across the field drowning out any chance of casual conversation by the crowd seated in the grandstand.

Off to my right, from the corner of my eye, I saw a giant of a knight swing his battle-ax downward straight into the center of a green shield with a wide red stripe running diagonally across the face. That shield saved its bearer from certain injury, if not death, from the skull-smashing force of the ax. The enormous knight, I knew, had to be Kevin. As he turned to engage another combatant, I could see a smile crease his face that was framed by his wildly flowing blond hair. The symbol of a silver hammer on a field of deep blue adorned his shield and convinced me that Kevin would make a valued addition to my team.

I turned to King Edgar but his attention was focused in the center of the field where a tall slender knight was surrounded by three others bent on taking him out of the competition.

A shield of light blue with a soaring eagle at the heart revealed that Garrett was in serious trouble, outnumbered three to one in a mock battle. As we watched, the three challengers seemed unsure as to their attack on a single warrior. Doubt, even for a split second, gave the quick-thinking Garrett all the time he needed. Stepping to his right, Garrett feigned a lunge toward the knight on that side. While the first knight flinched, the knight in the center brought down an overhead sword blow that Garrett blocked with his upraised shield. Dropping to one knee, Garrett spun and knocked down the third attacker with a perfectly timed backhand sword stroke. The knight that struck Garrett's shield had fallen off balance due to the force of his attack and was just gathering himself as Garrett swept his legs out from under him with his own outstretched leg as he continued his revolution. Two knights down, one left to go. Watching Garrett take out two knights with low sweeping movements, the first knight suddenly seemed unsure of himself. Clearly, he was young and badly outmanned. The young knight attempted an overhead stroke that seemed ill-advised considering the height advantage of his opponent. Easily blocked with an upraised shield, Garrett followed his block with a powerful lunge that knocked his foe off balance. A quick slash of his sword across the chest and Garrett's third attacker was out. Size, quickness, and wit all made Garrett an exceptional choice for my crew.

What began as approximately 100 well-armed and well-trained knights was quickly narrowed to what appeared to be fewer than 30.

To my left there seemed to be a bit of an uproar among a small circle of six men. In the center of the group was a knight, without a shield, whirling and slashing with both long and short sword. Quickness of foot and amazing skill with two blades gave away the identity of this knight. It was Sir Christopher who grew up on the shores of Lake Machnamh. Chris and another knight stood back to back in the center of a circle of combatants that seemed intent on putting them both out of the contest. As the two knights covered each other's back they slowly circled, looking for a weakness among the attackers closing in on them. Chris seemed to analyze each knight in turn, planning the best way to attack.

A green shield emblazoned with a brown bull's head, revealed that Ryan was the other knight in the center of the circle. I had been worried about Ryan's ability to succeed in this type of competition since his true area of expertise was with the longbow and, as the rules stated, no one was allowed to use a bow and arrow.

Chris and Ryan smartly had teamed together in the face of overwhelming odds. As the surrounding knights circled slowly, Chris struck without warning. The surprise caught one opponent off guard and that quick decision and sudden strike to the helmet assured the contest had one fewer knight. Following Chris' lead and relying on the surprise and indecision among their attackers, Ryan lunged with his green shield, smashing the knight directly in front of him right in the chest. Stunned, he dropped to his knee, coughing and trying to catch his breath, he was out of the battle.

Without waiting to see the result of his shield strike, in one continuous motion, Ryan spun quickly and, with the flat of his sword, slashed another knight across the side of his helmet, leaving three more knights for him and Chris to dispatch. One of the three remaining attackers recovered from the surprise of seeing three of his mates eliminated so quickly and chopped with an overhead strike of his sword attempting to put Chris out with one powerful stroke. Crossing his blades in an 'X' over his head, Chris caught his attacker's sword, twisted as quick as lightning, and jerked the sword from the knight's hand flinging it to the ground and out of reach. Uncrossing his blades, Chris slashed the disarmed knight on either side his helmet with the flat of both blades at the same time, sending him to the sideline with his comrades.

Spinning on his heel to face his final two opponents, Chris saw a flash of silver coming straight toward his head from the attacker on his right. Too late to react, Chris knew he was out. But, Ryan proved to be quicker, blocking the slashing blade with a thrust of his shield. Chris recovered to slash his assailant across the back.

Chris and Ryan turned as one to face their final opponent who, knowing he was outmanned, turned his sword in his hand, dropped to a knee, and offered his sword to his acknowledged superiors.

-27-

The afternoon sun was beginning to set which meant the tournament was drawing to a close. Colorful shields and pennants changed with the ending day to deeper, darker shades of their former selves. A red-orange glow lingered just above the trees of the nearby forest when King Edgar turned to me and asked, "Well, Nat, do you have your team?"

With that, I knew that I did and turned to King Edgar to tell him so. At a glance I realized that Charis was no longer in her seat on the other side of the king. A roar from the crowd drew my attention from Charis' empty chair and back to the far end of the tournament field.

Standing before a red and black striped tent was a gigantic knight armored all in black from head to toe. He, apparently, had been waiting in his tent to join the fight at the end, when only the best knights were still on the field. A red plume crowned his shiny black helmet, and a red cape fluttered behind him on the late afternoon breeze. In his right hand the black knight held a long black sword with a red jewel on the pommel. In his left he held a shield of black with a red oak tree emblazoned in the center.

A hush fell over the crowd as the giant in black stepped onto the tournament field to face the five remaining knights: Chase, Garrett, Kevin, Ryan, and Christopher. They looked exhausted from the competition and I wondered if they had enough energy left to defeat such a formidable foe.

Onto the field, stormed my mystery knight. He was a glorious sight, a blur of gleaming silver, like a bolt of lightning. Tall in the saddle, sword held aloft in his right hand, a plain white shield with painted red fox running across the center, in his left, and that fox-shaped helmet once again concealing his identity. His white horse sent turf flying into the air as it hurtled fearlessly toward the giant black knight.

The black knight turned to face the horseman, but too late. On the first pass a hard sword stroke unbalanced the black knight as it smashed against his black shield. Wheeling his horse quickly with the skill of a highly trained rider, sending turf and gravel flying, the horseman rammed his white shield squarely into the side of the black knight's head. Already staggered by the crushing blow, the black knight reeled at the quickness with which the mysterious knight dismounted and repeatedly hacked and slashed at the black knight with the flat of his sword. Finally, the defenseless black knight dropped both shield and sword to his sides and fell with a deafening thud to the tournament ground.

-28-

"Enough!" Bellowed King Edgar in his ever-powerful voice as a great flourish of trumpets signaled the end of the competition. The six remaining knights on the field turned to face King Edgar and the rest of the delighted crowd. I was beside myself with excitement that the six knights I had so painstakingly selected had proved themselves in combat. Mock combat though it was, their skills had been the difference in the tournament.

As my knights aligned themselves before the king, they all removed their helmets, all except, of course, the mystery knight.

"It is time to reveal yourself, Sir Knight," King Edgar boomed with a great smile on his face. Turning to me the king said, "Nat, there are many secrets that exist in a kingdom the size of Westerford."

I must have shown my confusion on my face for Edgar put a firm hand on my shoulder as he continued, "Some secrets are small and unimportant in the grand scheme of the kingdom, some are large, and the revealing of those large secrets may do great damage to the kingdom. And, some secrets must await the perfect moment to be unveiled."

With that a great gasp arose from the assembled crowd as King Edgar turned me by the shoulder to face the six knights poised before the king. As my eyes focused on the knights in front of me I scanned my team. Before me stood Sir Garrett, the traveler from the furthest end of the kingdom; Sir Kevin, the giant from the hill country to the north; Sir Christopher from the shores of Lake Machnamh; Sir Ryan, the cattle rancher from the foothills of Mount Uasal; Sir Chase, the blacksmith's son and skilled horseman; and, the mystery knight who leaned forward removing his helmet and shaking out his long, golden hair before standing straight and tall to reveal that he was not a "he" at all, but was, in fact, my beloved Charis.

When the initial shock of that secret had begun to wear off, King Edgar explained that, since she was a little girl growing up in the castle Charis had been trained in all manner of weaponry and battle strategy by the greatest instructors in the kingdom. Her training and skill at arms were kept secret from me until she felt certain that she had proved herself to me as well as the rest of the King's Guard Knights. It was important to Charis that she earn our respect and not be knighted simply because she was King Bert's daughter, King Edgar's niece and, especially, not because she was my wife.

I must admit there was a twinge of concern over Charis being one of my knights. She was, after all, my wife and I would hate for her status as a knight to put her into harm's way. When it came time to produce an heir to the throne of Westerford we would need to have a serious discussion about our future as knights. I knew that someday even I would not be able to continue on as a knight. As the future king I would be forced to take on a more protected, regal role. Although I would lead my knights fearlessly into battle if the cause were ever to arise, my days of traveling around the kingdom doing "knightly" duties were numbered. This would be the case with Charis as well. In the future, we would have to consider what was best for the kingdom. Putting the king and queen of Westerford into danger as knights would seem to go against that philosophy.

There was no doubt in my mind that these six knights were my choice to lead the King's Guard and train as the elite unit within the Guard. I turned to King Edgar as the sun sank below the Westerford horizon and said, with a bow, "My Lord, with your permission, I'd like to invite the knights before you to join me in training as members of the team you tasked me to assemble." With a sweep of my arm I pointed to the knights before us and continued, "Before today's competition, King Edgar, I had already recognized these knights for their skill at arms as well as the respect they command among their peers."

King Edgar nodded in agreement as I continued, "Of course I did not know that Charis was my mystery knight, although her skills and work ethic set her apart from most of her fellow knights. It doesn't matter to me one bit that she is a woman, other than the fact she is my wife," I said with a slight laugh. King Edgar burst into laughter at my little joke and said, "Your attitude toward women is refreshing, Nat. But, the fact that Charis is your wife, a princess, and the future queen of Westerford, doesn't give you pause to select her as one of you team?" The king asked with a suddenly serious tone.

"Your Majesty," I continued with an equally serious tone, "I was asked to observe the knights of the King's Guard during training to choose six knights with qualities that I deemed important for those knights to possess in order for us to work together to become an elite fighting unit as well as a team fit to represent Your Majesty throughout the kingdom. The fact that Charis is a woman, my wife, the princess, and future queen of Westerford was not a factor when I didn't know that she was the mystery knight and I don't think it should matter now. In fact, I think that she will serve as a perfect example of what one can achieve, whether man or woman, with hard work and training. Charis, as proved by her swift dismantling of that mountain of a black knight, belongs among the elite knights that I've selected," I finished decisively.

"Very well," King Edgar said, "I would like to invite these knights you've chosen to a feast in their honor tonight in my Great Hall. They should be honored for their skill as demonstrated in the tournament today and I would like to spend some time getting to know them. Also, there is the matter of the "Champion's Medal" and 20 gold pieces."

The knights, still standing before the grandstand, bowed deeply to show their respect and gratitude to King Edgar for his generosity.

"King Edgar," I said, "With your permission, we have one stop to make before we join you at the feast."

Edgar was clearly surprised to be put off, though just briefly since he already knew my reason for the delay. With a knowing gleam in his eye and a smile on his face he said, "I remember the reason for your delay. The full moon is rising over Mount Uasal and you have an appointment to keep."

With that it was my turn to wear a surprised look on my face. As we rose to descend the grandstand steps, King Edgar patted me on the back and laughed, "My boy, it is the king's job to know what is happening in his kingdom. Take your knights to Blackie's shop and return to the Great Hall. I'm sure you want to get to work, but you've got to eat and I need to learn as much as I can about this talented group you've assembled."

-29-

With the king's vote of confidence, we seven knights mounted our horses and kicked them into a gallop toward Sutter and Blackie's shop. I looked toward the evening sky and saw Danby soaring above us silhouetted against the bright full moon.

A golden glow of firelight spilled through the windows of Blackie's humble cottage and oozed into the empty street as we slowed our horses to a trot before coming to a stop. As one, we dismounted and Chase burst through the front door as he had done a million times before and hugged his mother tightly. He took a quick taste of whatever she was cooking in the black iron pot hanging above the fire that glowed bright orange on the hearth. In the back of the house was Blackie's forge where he formed raw metals into farm tools, weapons, kitchen utensils, and armor. We were there for armor and eagerly followed Chase through the house and out back into the outdoor workspace.

The "Smithy" was an open area where Blackie's forge burned with intense heat and his anvil rang daily with the rhythmic song of the blacksmith. Behind the forge was a large enclosure that housed a storage area and workshop. We knocked on the wooden workshop door and waited for Blackie to answer.

-30-

Funny to think back now, but butterflies danced around in my stomach waiting to see what Chase's father had created for us. The worn oaken door creaked open to reveal the blacksmith, tall and strong. His face permanently darkened from years at the forge, a gray shirt, that once was white, draped his giant shoulders and the sleeves were rolled up above muscled forearms and biceps. Behind Blackie was a warm room that appeared to be occupied by a band of knights. Of course the craftsman had finished the armor and arranged it on posts to appear as though armored soldiers stood at the ready in his workshop. I quickly counted seven coats-of-arms and realized that King Edgar had known that Charis would earn the seventh spot on my team and sent her to Blackie for measurements.

I stood in the doorway, dumbfounded, unable to say a word, my whole being focused on the gleaming soldiers staring back at me from inside the shop. When I was finally able to look away from the brilliant armor, I saw Blackie smiling broadly, obviously proud of his work. I stepped into the workshop and hugged Blackie tightly with both arms and whispered, "Thank you," into his ear before I released my grip pulling away with a tear in my eye. Blackie patted me on the back with his strong blacksmith's hand and kept his arm around me as he walked me to the center of the workshop among the suits of armor.

Something was odd, or just a bit different about the armor. At closer inspection the armor appeared to glow with a greenish-blue tint that appeared to have scales – like a dragon! I couldn't contain my excitement. Hugging Blackie, I asked about the beautiful armor and how he created that amazing color.

"I've been working with new combinations of metals," he said. "Several months ago I was able to make a blend that was harder and stronger than the regular steel we've always used for armor. Turned out that metal was also lighter," he explained. "The only downside to the new alloy – or so I first thought – was this strange greenish-blue glow it gave off. When you and your knights came to me for new armor I knew just what to do. Rumors of an elite group of knights have been circulating wildly around the kingdom and it seems that everyone has already heard of you – the intense training and unmatched skills you have. We also know that you travel in the company of Danby, the only known dragon. So, I thought, what better armor for you than the strongest, lightest armor in the whole kingdom? I fashioned the helmets with the shape of Danby's horns on them so, if the color wasn't enough, the whole kingdom would recognize the 'Dragon Knights,'" he finished.

-31-

As I made my way around the room looking at each suit of armor carefully I noticed that on the breastplate of the armor was etched with an artist's skill a different "runic" symbol. I chased away my usual feeling of frustration at not knowing the ancient symbols or their meaning and, curiously asked, "What is the significance of these runes?"

Without a word from Blackie, my teacher, Ollamh, stepped out from behind one of the metallic soldiers.

"Maybe he can tell you," said Blackie softly as he stepped aside giving Ollamh the floor.

In his musical tone Ollamh began to explain, "Sir Nathaniel, the addition of the runic symbols was my idea and each symbol is unique and descriptive of the suit's wearer."

"Step forward, please, Sir Garrett," Ollamh said turning to the tall knight. As Garrett stepped toward an equally tall suit of armor Ollamh explained, "Garrett you are the eldest of the 'Dragon Knights' and have traveled far and wide throughout the kingdom during your years with the King's Guard. Your rune 'ᚱ' is the symbol for a 'ride' or 'journey' and represents your life experience as a traveler and soldier." Without pausing for comment, Ollamh left Garrett to admire his new gear and put his arm around the next knight's broad shoulders.

"Sir Kevin," Ollamh led the powerful knight to a matching metal suit. "Your rune is the symbol for the legendary god Thor. 'ᚦ' representing 'strength' just as your power represents the Kingdom of Westerford." Kevin nodded his thanks to Ollamh and lightly fingered the grooved lines of the 'ᚦ' on his breastplate.

"Sir Ryan," Ollamh called the archer and directed him to the armor with an 'ᚠ' etched deeply on the chest. "This rune you should have seen before," Ryan nodded but his face still bore a look of wonder as he reached out to touch the carving. "Your family has been cattle ranchers in the foothills of Mount Uasal for generations. The 'ᚠ' represents 'wealth' and 'cattle' just as on your family crest." Ryan smiled and nodded slightly, knowing that his rune was a perfect tribute to his family name.

"Sir Chase, your rune is the symbol 'ᛖ' and represents the 'horses' that you grew up among and control with a level of equestrian expertise unequalled in our kingdom or any other," Ollamh explained. Stepping quickly from Chase to Sir Christopher, he began again, "Chris you grew up on the shores of Lake Machnamh and your skill in and around water is beyond compare. But, you also battle with a speed and fluidity that reflects your childhood on the water. Therefore, your rune, 'ᛚ', is the symbol for 'lake' representing both your home and your fighting style."

With only two coats of armor left Charis and I stood hand-in-hand facing our armor. Ollamh gently took Charis by her free hand and led her to the smallest suit matching her petite and distinctly feminine form. "Charis, Princess of Westerford, your runic symbol is 'ᛈ' which is the rune for 'joy.' I chose this rune for you simply because you have brought so much joy to so many in our kingdom." Charis smiled broadly then her smile softened as her fingers traced the symbol. I knew, at that moment that Charis was thinking of her father, King Bert, and Queen Veronica, the mother she never knew.

"Finally, Sir Nathaniel," Ollamh turned to me, "you have lived a charmed life as evidenced by your best friend, Danby, your rise to knighthood from humble origins, your successful completion of the King's Quest, and your marriage to our lovely Princess Charis." I nodded my agreement with Ollamh's assessment of my fortunate life knowing that without Danby none of the other treasures would have come my way. "Your rune is the symbol 'ᚲᛋ' which is the mark for 'gift.' There is no arguing that you have been blessed with a glorious gift, Nat. But, many people are given gifts that are wasted. You, my young friend, have used your gift to do what is good and right. Therefore, the symbol '⟨ϟ' will forever remind you of your great gift every time you don this armor in the name of Westerford, King Edgar, and the noble 'Dragon Knights.'"

I bowed my head, overwhelmed with a feeling of deep respect and honor. After a pause to collect myself, I said, "Thank you, Ollamh. Your wisdom and thoughtfulness have been valuable lessons to us tonight and will continue to guide us as long as we wear the uniform of the 'Dragon Knights.'"

With that, I turned to my six companions and said, "My friends, we have been personally invited to a feast, in our honor, by our king, in the Great Hall at Westerford Castle. I'd say they've waited long enough. Let's put on our new armor and ride to the castle as King Edgar's 'Dragon Knights.'"

We armed ourselves in our new and finely fitted gear, bid goodbye to Blackie and Ollamh, and, with Danby gliding overhead as we rode, made our way as one, to our feast at Westerford Castle. Each of us knowing, in our minds, that this was the first of many times we would ride together.

From that day forward, we were known as the Dragon Knights of Westerford. We were a band of brothers with one mission: to live a knightly life. We were honest, faithful and brave. Loyal to king and kingdom, we studied hard and were ever vigilant – looking for others in need of help and doing whatever we could do to help them.

THE TRUE DRAGON KING

-1-

I woke with a start. Lying in my large comfortable bed I reached beside me and felt Charis sleeping soundly. Her soft breathing had become familiar and I smiled at the thought of having her by my side for the rest of my life.

Without a sound I slid from beneath the covers and padded silently to the tall window across the room. Easing the thick curtain aside I looked over our kingdom from high above in the castle.

Still, in the middle of the night, there was not much to see. A bright half-moon gave a silvery shine to the treetops in the forest. Closer, dull orange firelight spilled into the street from the windows of cottages in the village below.

As I turned to creep back to the warmth of my bed a reddish-orange glow in the distance caught my eye. It seemed to be coming from somewhere in the farthest corner of the forest. A glow of that color and size could only be made by a huge bonfire. I had explored miles and miles of trails in Tranglam Forest in recent months but, admittedly, had never been all the way to that far part where the glow came from. The locals called that area of Tranglam Forest "Dorchadas" or darkness, as in "the forces of darkness" or evil. While I admit the idea of exploring an area labeled "evil" didn't really appeal to me, I felt no fear at the prospect of exploring the Dorchadas.

I closed the curtains and quietly slipped back into my warm bed, gave Charis a gentle kiss on the cheek, and tumbled off to sleep with plans for a new adventure racing through my head.

-2-

Every night just before dinnertime 100 members of the King's Guard would meet in the Great Hall with King Edgar. Most of these meetings were spent discussing news of the kingdom. The knights of the King's Guard patrolled the kingdom as part of a constant rotation. Fifty knights in the castle for protection and 50 in the field. They never patrolled as a show of force or police action, the King's Guard's role was a positive one. They would visit villages to make sure all was well and lend a hand where one was needed. It was another way to help the people of the kingdom feel safe – they knew the King's Guard was watching out for them and that the whole kingdom mattered.

Upon returning from a patrol, each knight would report to King Edgar about where they had gone. They would discuss the people they met and the places they had seen while out on patrol. Usually the reports were pretty basic. A knight may have visited three villages, talked to some farmers about their crops, the weather, even the price of grain at market. Perhaps he helped a merchant repair a wagon wheel on the side of the road or stopped to play ball or "knights" with a group of children. Another duty the King's Guard had while on patrol was to listen to complaints or judge minor problems. Of course anything major that could not be easily resolved in the field would be reported to the king and brought before his high council. Fortunately, there were not many problems that the King's Guard could not resolve. But, one such complaint caused a stir that rocked the kingdom to its core and started an adventure that changed the realm forever.

-3-

Summer in Westerford had been as mild as anyone could remember. Blue skies, green meadows and not a care in the world. Charis and I were happy together. We never really got to know each other before my quest. It was more a mutual case of "love at first sight." Many older members of the king's court whispered that our love would never last. In fact, Charis and I became fast friends during the few months between my successful adventures and our wedding. We spent hours together, every day, always accompanied by her ladies-in-waiting of course. Even with extra eyes and ears observing our every moment together we fell madly in love.

Our wedding ceremony was held on the first day of that glorious spring. A clearing in the forest, like a cathedral beneath a ceiling of overarching branches, was decorated with bright flowers and colored streamers. It created an explosion of color splashed among the deep browns and greens of the surrounding forest. Bright finger-like beams from the springtime sun found their way through the treetops to light the forest floor around us. Looking up, I was able to catch a glimpse of blue sky laced with wispy clouds smiling above the ceremony.

I recall the priest saying something about our marriage being fresh and new like the spring day around us. But, all I really remember for sure was my beautiful bride gently holding my hands and my smiling face reflected in her blue eyes. All I wanted, from that moment on, was to always be the reflection in those eyes. Magical is the only word I could come up with to describe that day.

-4-

Springtime melted into that perfect mild summer and Charis and I were bound forever. Autumn erupted in a pallet of colors – oranges, reds, yellows and browns – as the whole countryside prepared for a bountiful harvest.

It happened one evening during harvest time as a full moon lit up the night sky. It was while Danby and I soared around the castle and high above the village taking one last look around before bedtime, that I saw her hobbling down the old road leading from Tranglam Forest toward the castle. I couldn't guess who would be walking alone on the isolated forest road at that hour. I signaled Danby back to the castle so that I might alert the King's Guard that a guest was approaching on the forest road toward the castle gate.

The courtyard was aglow with torchlight as I strode toward the portcullis to greet our late night guest. Curiosity, more than anything else, spurred my quick reaction to this lone visitor. I wondered who it could be, of course, but a strange sensation in the pit of my stomach gave me pause to think that this lone visitor was bringing trouble to the kingdom.

Hooded in an ink-black cloak, I could not see our guest's shadowed face. A crooked hand held a crooked wooden walking stick. I could see animal faces carved on the stick she was depending on for support. It was obvious that our visitor was old. My concern was, what business did this old, crooked stranger have at Westerford Castle so late at night?

"Good evening, and welcome to Westerford Castle," I made to greet the stranger as I would welcome any guest. But, I still had a chill of apprehension as I approached and offered to remove the stranger's cloak. Swiftly and with unexpected strength the crooked walking stick knocked my hand away from the cloak.

"I need no assistance from you, my boy," was the curt, response from the stranger. "I've come to meet with King Edgar. I have urgent business that will not wait until morning." Another crooked hand reached up from beneath the ink-black cloak and pushed back the hood to reveal the face of a woman that had seen many, many years. Lines upon wrinkles etched her ancient face and accented her deep-set lifeless black eyes as they reflected the torchlight. A long, crooked nose was the centerpiece of her face and drew attention away from the cluster of whiskers growing from her pointy chin. Bushy gray eyebrows as unruly as the hair on her chin reached out at all angles over her eyes. All this was topped with a stringy nest of dirty gray hair that had the consistency of dead straw.

The urgency in her voice was overshadowed only by her anger. I really didn't know what to do; I decided to learn more before sending a squire to awaken Gregory, King Edgar's steward, to rouse the king with news of our guest.

"And, who should my squire announce as our visitor?" I asked as kindly as I could. Looking me squarely in the eye and pointing a crooked finger in my direction, the old woman cackled, "My name is Talia and I live free in the Forest Tranglam. It is urgent that I see King Edgar. He is in grave danger. Only I know from where it comes."

With that, I signaled my squire to awaken Gregory with the new information so that King Edgar could receive Talia's warning. I invited Talia into the Great Hall to get out of the cold night air. She seemed to smile when a large bowl of steaming stew was placed in front of her at the table. She spoke to no one, but looked around suspiciously as servants and other members of the court passed in and out of the Great Hall. Talia refused to remove her cloak and even kept her hood on her head while she ate. Though a bit rude in most circles, no one thought it any more odd than a lone old woman walking all the way from Tranglam Forest to Westerford Castle at night with an urgent message of warning for the king.

-5-

The whole situation seemed strange and gave me a bad feeling as I awaited King Edgar. I was more than a little curious to know what could possibly be so urgent that it could not wait until morning.

I met the king in the antechamber behind the throne in the Great Hall. Expansive tapestries hid King Edgar's two personal bodyguards and the door to the chamber. We were safe to talk there. Explaining the arrival of Talia so late at night made me feel as though waking the king might not have been the wisest move on my part. But, when I spoke Talia's name, a look of terror flushed King Edgar's face. I knew the king had the same uneasy feeling that I did.

Rising from his chair, King Edgar nodded to the door and said, "It's time to meet this forest witch to hear her 'urgent message.'"

Although "witch" was the name that crossed my mind when I first saw Talia, the king saying it out loud made my uneasy feelings all the more real.

I led the way as we opened the chamber door to enter the Great Hall. As we made our way to the dais, I bowed, giving King Edgar due respect as he ascended to sit on his throne. As he sat down, I glanced up at the brightly colored tapestries hanging around the walls. They told the stories of all the great, and not-so-great, leaders and heroes throughout Westerford's history. King Edgar, I thought, would surely be remembered among the greatest for his wisdom, bravery and the love he had for his people.

Glancing toward the long, oaken feasting tables at the back of the hall, I noticed that Talia had neither risen nor looked up from her stew when the king entered the hall. What was her urgent message? I could not imagine.

Taking his place on the throne, King Edgar, in his booming voice – he was a giant of a man – called to Talia, "Talia of Tranglam Forest, keeper of the wood and all her creatures, great and small, to what do we owe your late-night visit? What 'urgent message' do you have that caused you to walk from your warm home in the Dorchadas all the way to Westerford Castle? It must be of utmost importance since it could not even wait until morning."

Rising to her full height, which wasn't very tall at all, and still cloaked in black, her head still covered by her hood, Talia slowly made her way, leaning heavily on her crooked walking stick, to the dais steps, never looking at King Edgar until she was right in front of him. When Talia lifted her head to address the king there was a glow in her eyes that was not a reflection from the Great Hall's fire or torches. Anger in her eyes screamed danger for King Edgar. Before anyone could move to defend the king, Talia drew what appeared to be a dagger carved of glass from within the folds of her cloak. As though flying, Talia was upon the king, driving her glass dagger, to the hilt, into King Edgar's chest.

Time seemed to stand still as I watched this witch viciously attack Edgar. No one moved to help him. I realized that I could not move. I could see and hear everything that was happening but could do nothing about it.

Talia stepped back from the throne, raised both hands up high, still holding her crooked walking stick, smoke and fire seemed to fly from her fingertips as she spoke. Her voice loud and crackling, made a sing-song tune as she swayed back and forth never taking her glowing eyes off of King Edgar who sat pale and dazed on his throne, the clear handle of Talia's dagger sticking out of his chest. I found it odd at that terrifying moment that no blood showed on the king's chest. But, I shook off the feeling and swiftly focused on the words coming from Talia's mouth:

Where fire and ice together dwell
Deep within a Tranglam Dell,
Standing stones dance round a throne,
Made for One True King alone.
My curse upon your kingly head,
Shall leave you neither live nor dead.
Upon your throne both day and night
You'll sit, too weak to stand or fight.
Until a knight can solve my riddle
You'll hover somewhere in the middle
World between life and death,
And struggle taking every breath.
My riddle may sound simple here
Much more there is than meets the ear.
Across the morning sky they soar,
Never flying there before.
From common blood a knight ascends,
A mythic creature he befriends,
And takes a maid lovely and fair,
Becoming both husband and heir.
Days gone by in hollow tree
A giant egg hid golden key.
When the egg at last was found,
Two in one at last were bound.
The golden key you must uncover,
What it unlocks you must discover.
Hidden by a liquid curtain,
What lies there still? No one is certain.
It dwells behind a wall of stone
Where once were found both gold and bone.
Through the tunnel, cross the floor,
Dying sunlight shows the door.
When it is found, no need to knock,
Use the key, unlock the lock,
Push the door, step in with care,
What you seek is down the stair.

Descend the stairway all alone,
And there you'll find an oaken throne.
Among the roots you'll find a drawer,
Where no one thought to look before.
If truly you will be a king
You first must find the golden ring,
Forged when our kingdom first began
And worn by rulers of this land.
Great power holds the ring of gold,
It is the One True King's to hold.
To save the king from darkest hour
You must unleash a greater power.
When slipped upon the True King's finger,
His majesty will cease to linger
'Tween the living and the dead
The crown once more atop his head.
Its power only saves the king –
Find the key to find the ring.

When the words ceased, Talia lowered her hands, once again becoming the crooked old woman that I saw walking toward the castle on the forest road. She bent forward and leaned heavily on her crooked walking stick. Rage boiled my blood. I could move again, but being unarmed, since no one carried weapons in the Great Hall, I moved to protect the king with my body. Too late, I thought, this dagger strike would surely be fatal.

From the corner of my eye I saw the king's sword, Cumhacht, hanging on the throne in its brightly adorned scabbard. With one swift movement I drew Cumhacht by the jewel-encrusted hilt, and with a backhand sweep I struck Talia squarely on the neck. I fully expected her head to fly cleanly from her shoulders and across the Great Hall. Without a sound Talia's cloak fell to the floor, an empty pile of black cloth. In a blink, Talia was gone.

-6-

Everyone froze in place. A stunned silence filled the Great Hall. True to the curse, King Edgar sat upon his throne unable to move or even speak above a feeble whisper.

Standing over Talia's black cloak, I looked down to discover a tightly rolled parchment among the rumpled cloth. I carefully unrolled the fragile paper to discover that Talia had left behind a transcript of her curse. "She wants me to save Edgar," I thought to myself as I read over the words that chilled me to my very core. As heir to the throne, leader of the King's Guard and, obviously one of the prime subjects of Talia's curse, I decided I must act quickly.

I called to the king's steward, Gregory. He'd been in the antechamber and was at my side in a flash. I told him to fetch Edgar's personal surgeon to discover what, if anything, could be done. Next, I called for the King's Guard. I assigned four knights to maintain a 24-hour vigil on the four corners of King Edgar's throne where, according to the curse, he was destined to remain until the riddle could be solved. No one, save the surgeon and nurses, was to approach the king in his current condition. Finally, I called my "Dragon Knights" together to formulate a plan. Danby joined us in the Great Hall and listened as I explained the curse and the quest we were about to begin. When Sir Kevin asked what was to be done about Talia, I replied, simply, "Restoring King Edgar's health and his rightful place as King of Westerford is the most important thing right now. Talia, I'm sure, has used her magic to return to her home in the forest. First, the king, then, the witch."

Nothing more was spoken about Talia by the Dragon Knights. We had a dangerous quest, an adventure far more serious than any before. And, the future of our king and kingdom depended completely on us.

-7-

At first light, as our squires packed our supplies, the Dragon Knights donned their deep blue-green armor, checked their weapons and bid their loved ones goodbye. A single tear rolled down Charis' cheek and I brushed it away with the back of my hand and whispered, "Don't despair. We will solve this riddle and save your uncle." She knew the importance of our journey. And, she knew we would not fail. Charis kissed me gently on the lips and, looking deeply into my eyes said, "I love you, Nathaniel." She waved goodbye to her ladies-in-waiting and the many other courtiers who had assembled to see us off as she put on her helmet and mounted her horse. With Danby circling overhead, we rode side-by-side through the castle gates leading the rest of the Dragon Knights across the ancient wooden drawbridge. Our quest: to save King Edgar and restore our peaceful kingdom.

Leading my Dragon Knights to where I found Danby's egg was easy. Although the dense ground cover and rotting tree falls made travel tricky, I knew that path as well as any road I had ever traveled. Danby seemed excited to return to the place of his youth. This hollow tree was his home until I revealed his existence and we moved to the castle. King Edgar had built a special structure of stone that was Danby's home. It was designed to look like a cave beneath the side of the castle wall, but was finished and finely decorated by the king's best craftsmen as a home for a very special member of the kingdom.

The green of the forest floor, broken by gray and brown moss, fallen logs and a tumble of rocks was made even more beautiful by the hundreds of sunbeams that poked their way through the ancient forest canopy creating a maze of intersecting shadows on the forest floor.

One small stream to cross, a short climb up a hill; the next dell would reveal Danby's former home. Excitement made me giggle as I hurried to crest that last hill. To the other Knights, it was nothing more than an old hollow tree lying on the forest floor. A look of confused disappointment replaced the smiles of my companions. They just didn't understand how important this simple scene was to me. I loved this place. As quick as a flash, I dismounted from my horse. Handing the reins to Chase, I jumped onto Danby's back and, without warning to the rest, my best friend and I were airborne soaring the last 100 yards as we had done a thousand times before. We came in low and fast over the top of the hollow log, saw the opening was exactly as we had left it, cut hard to our right, and turned straight up. Through a gap in the trees overhead we shot into the open sky above. It was just as blue as it always seemed to be during those early flights from my childhood.

Reaching our favorite elevation, high above the trees, we could see for miles in every direction. We both wanted to fly on forever. But, King Edgar and the whole kingdom were in mortal danger. It was up to us to somehow find the key to unlock Talia's riddle.

With slight pressure from my right knee Danby knew that we had work to do. Without wasting another moment he rolled to the left, away from the pressure of my knee, and we spun into a dive back to his old forest home. We leveled out just a few feet above the forest floor and, with a final beat of Danby's great wings, we came to rest on top of his fallen log where the rest of my Dragon Knights awaited the next step of our journey.

Smiling slightly to hide her worry for the king, Charis asked, "Where do you think the key might be, Nat?" Still breathless from my exhilarating flight, I unrolled Talia's parchment and said, "The riddle says, 'a giant egg hid golden key.' Danby lived here for a few years after he hatched but I don't remember ever doing any digging inside the hollow log where I found the egg." With that I put the parchment back into my knapsack and we all climbed into the giant log to dig for the golden key. Once inside the log Chris asked, in his typically quizzical way, "Where, exactly, was the egg when you found it?"

Turning around to get my bearings, and looking up to see the hole I had originally fallen through, I pointed to the exact place on the floor where the egg had been partially buried. Even after the intervening years, there was still an obvious indentation in the moss-littered ground.

Without a thought Ryan and Kevin fell to ground and desperately began digging, carefully trying to expose whatever might be buried beneath the spot where I had first discovered Danby's egg.

A silent anticipation and excitement seemed to fill the hollow log as Garrett, Chase, Chris, Charis and I watched, holding our breath, as Ryan and Kevin carefully turned over the moist, dark soil handfuls at a time.

Suddenly, Kevin let out a groan and said, "Ow! I've just scraped my fingers on a rock or something buried here." While Kevin pulled back to assess the damage, Ryan continued more slowly moving aside handfuls of dirt to find the sides of the rock Kevin had discovered.

Soon Ryan traced the outline, not of a rock, but squared corners and straight edges of a stone box. Drawing his knife, Ryan dug deeper along the edges until he was able to pry the entire box from the hole.

About six inches long and four inches across, the box was carved with the picture of a dragon soaring over a great oak tree. Intricate detail framed the dragon and tree with several runic figures filling the box's frame – how many times would I wish I understood the ancient symbols?

I held the stone box in both hands and tried to lift the lid. No matter how hard I pulled, the box would not open. Frustrated, I was just about to throw the box down against a rock to shatter it. But, before I could, Chase calmly suggested, "Why don't you try sliding the lid?" Sure enough, as usual, frustration was not the answer, logic was. Holding the box in both hands, I pressed the lid with my thumbs. As easy as that the beautiful box slid open revealing a golden key etched with the same runes and the same dragon and oak tree.

Charis stood and removed a thick golden chain from around her neck. With an approving nod from me, she took the key from the box and fastened it securely to the chain. Leaning over me she placed the chain and key around my neck and tucked it inside my armor for safekeeping.

Standing quickly I said, "Time to go to Dragon Veil Falls!" With one voice my whole team asked, "What's in Dragon Veil Falls?"

"Legend says that there is cursed treasure hidden in secret caves behind the falls," began Chase with an obviously shaken tone in his voice.

"Laighart, the dragon, made his home behind the falls. Hoarding his riches – gold and jewels – deep in his lair. The older villagers say that he would drag his human victims into the dark tunnels and devour them, while lying on his pile of treasure, discarding their bones among the loot," Chris added with the confidence of someone with firsthand knowledge.

"The next part of the riddle says that this key unlocks something 'hidden by a liquid curtain,'" I said excitedly. "I have been inside the tunnels behind Dragon Veil Falls," I continued, "and I have found 'both gold and bone' just as the curse says. Dragon Veil Falls and the tunnels hidden behind the falls must be where I'll find the ring that will save King Edgar," I said firmly, knowing exactly what to do next.

As one, and without another thought, the Dragon Knights rose and climbed out of the giant hollow log ready to explore the storied tunnels behind Dragon Veil Falls at the far end of Lake Machnamh.

At last I decided to put the rumors and legends to rest once and for all. "As I said, I have explored the caves behind Dragon Veil Falls myself," I began. "It is true that there is an unimaginable hoard of wealth hidden deep within the ancient tunnels. When I was there, many years ago, I filled my knapsack with enough gold to support my quest to become a knight. I really didn't believe in the curse anyway. But, the way I figured it, as long as I was using the treasure for good and noble causes I would be safe from the curse. So far, there have been no ill effects of taking a small share of the dragon's cache," I finished as I swiftly climbed onto my horse and began making my way through the thick forest in the direction of Dragon Veil Falls.

"Wait for us!" shouted the rest of the knights as they, too, mounted their horses to follow me.

Once we had mounted our horses we began the trek through the forest that bordered the lake. The trail was clearly marked, but the forest was dense and it took several hours to pick our way around the long lake. With Danby soaring overhead keeping watch we would reach the base of Dragon Veil Falls long before sunset when, according to the riddle, the "Dying sunlight shows the door." Keeping Lake Machnamh on our right side we told stories and sang songs to help pass the time and hide our nervousness. Danby entertained us by diving into the lake from high above only to resurface with a mouthful of fresh fish. We cheered and laughed each time he emerged dripping wet from the cool waters of Lake Machnamh. He was a nice distraction from the serious nature of our quest. But deep down we all could picture our beloved king sprawled on his throne with the glass knife protruding from his chest.

-8-

Approaching Dragon Veil Falls was much less frightening than it was my first time. Talia obviously had no idea that anyone had ever been into the cave behind the waterfall. I picked up on that part of her riddle right away. Of course, there was plenty of the riddle that still left me wondering. But, that would have to wait. For now my goal, and the goal of my band of Dragon Knights, was focused on locating the ring in the ancient throne room and saving King Edgar from Talia's curse.

Dismounting from our horses, we left Danby to guard them from wild animals in a meadow at the edge of the forest while we walked the last mile of trail through the thick haze created by Dragon Veil Falls. A frothing mist billowed like a giant cloud at the base of the falls where tons of tumbling water crashed toward Lake Machnamh only to explode on the jagged rocks below creating a massive wall of white that obscured the point where the falls met the lake. It was a powerful and awe-inspiring sight that few men and certainly not the rest of the Dragon Knights had never seen before. Struck silent, with mouths open wide with awe, I had to encourage my team to continue on through the mist until we could reach the winding stair that climbed the sheer cliff face.

It seemed like such a long time since I first discovered those beautifully carved stairs that wound their way up the damp cliff face. I wondered, as I led my Dragon Knights up that magical stairway, how long ago they had been etched into that sheer rock wall. Who had the skill to create such a remarkable work of art? As we made our way up those long, winding stairs I looked carefully at the detail with which they had been carved. Each step was decorated with different designs: some were swirls; some were cloud-like; some looked like strange animals; and some were even carved to resemble heavenly bodies – stars, moons, and the sun. All of the tiny carvings were so detailed that I struggled to imagine how long it must have taken the artists to complete these stairs, and we hadn't even reached the caves yet!

No one said a word as we worked our way up the carved staircase. The rest of my team must have been as impressed as I to see such amazing detail crafted so long ago. The conversation finally began again as we all entered the enormous cave that opened up just behind the roaring curtain of Dragon Veil Falls. It was damp in this part of the cave, just as I remembered it. But, through some engineering magic, it wasn't nearly as loud as I thought it should be.

Having walked single file so far, from our final trek through the woods and all the way up the zigzagging stairs, this was the perfect place to regroup and plan the next part of our quest. Everyone carried extra provisions for the journey. Chase and Garrett carried the mess kits that included plates and silverware in addition to a large tarp that could be spread on the ground as a "tablecloth" for us to eat our meals. Our "meal" today consisted of bread, hard cheese and water. We had learned to travel light during our training and this was a perfect example of it. Breakfast and lunch were always on the lighter side. Dinner was the meal when we would have meat, if we could find it, and some wild fruit or vegetables too.

Pulling out the tightly rolled parchment I read the next part of Talia's curse, "Hidden by a liquid curtain." The "liquid curtain" was obviously Dragon Veil Falls since it hides the caves where I found the gold and jewels and bones that filled the dragon's lair. "It dwells behind a wall of stone, where once were found both gold and bone," I continued. Without thinking about it I reached up to feel the golden key hanging on its chain around my neck. Soon I would have to leave my companions to find the golden ring "all alone." I don't know if the word "frightened" described my feelings accurately. But, having seen what Talia did to King Edgar, I was wary of what dangers might await me in the depths of the ancient chamber.

"It's nearly sunset," I said to the others who were lying around the cave, resting from their travels. We had covered many miles to reach the falls and, although it was fine company, we all carried the additional burden of worry about King Edgar. Charis, having been raised by her uncle, felt it more deeply than any of us, as a child worries for a sick parent. As we traveled we talked and laughed, told stories and sang songs, but deep down we all ached with the burden of what might happen if we failed.

"The curse tells us that the 'dying sunlight shows the door' so we should enter the treasure room and position ourselves for what comes next. We don't know how clearly the door will show or how long it will last," I voiced my concerns and looked at my companion's faces seeking some reassurance. Chris suggested that we form a circle in the room with our backs to the treasure to better see all the chamber's walls. "That way," he went on, "when the door appears we can shout out and Nat can hurry with the key to open it before it disappears again."

"That's an excellent plan, Chris," said Garrett, adding, "perhaps Nat should stand at the ready with the key in his hand, not looking for the door himself, so that he can move more quickly when one of us calls. If you are focused on one part of the wall it may take an extra tick of the clock to realize someone else has discovered the door. That brief amount of time might make all the difference."

With that I said, "Brilliant plan. The sun has begun to set so it is time for us to get in position. Remember, when we get into the chamber you may be distracted by the gold and jewels that are piled high in the center. It is quite impressive and will take discipline to maintain focus on our quest. Saving King Edgar is our priority now. Someday we will return to collect our shares." We quickly packed our things but left our bags where we had eaten. All that we carried with us were the unlit torches that Charis, in her ever-sensible way, suggested we might need inside the caves once the sun fully set. The tunnels, though masterfully carved with exquisite detail, were narrow so there was really no need to pack our bags in with us.

The outer cave glowed orange and red with the dying sun. Somehow it seemed to grow brighter in the chamber. Perhaps the waterfall magnified the sunlight in some way. Whatever the case, we could easily see the three tunnel entrances and I led the way toward the third tunnel. Knowing that the third opening led to the treasure room, I glanced up at the intricately carved runes above the doorway again wishing I understood the ancient written language. I counted seven distinct runic symbols carved above the doorway as I started down the winding tunnel but, once again, I couldn't read the word that the runes spelled. As we rounded the last turn in the tunnel and spilled into the treasure room I saw the same glow I remembered from so long ago. The treasure captured and reflected every beam of sunlight that made its way into the cave, and reflected it a thousand ways creating what appeared to be its own light source.

Once again, mouths dropped open with awe at the splendor of the treasure room. At least 100 feet across, the Dragon Knights would have to spread out around the mountain of treasure and scan the curved walls just to be able to spot the door when the setting sun revealed the outline on the wall. Gold and jewels and, yes, some dusty gray bones, were piled nearly to the ceiling in the center of the perfectly round room. The walls were decorated with runic writing and elegant murals depicting magical creatures carved into detailed forest scenes with sprawling trees, rolling hills, and wild running streams. It was curious to notice that there were no people in the pictures.

As quickly as we entered the treasure room, the Dragon Knights took their places facing the curved walls leaving about 10 feet of space between them. Their discipline was truly remarkable since even I had difficulty pulling my attention away from the mound of treasure and this wasn't my first time seeing it! I fumbled a bit removing the key from around my neck. Afraid I would drop it, I wound the chain around my hand holding the key firmly between my thumb and index finger. I was poised to spring toward the first knight to call out when they saw the door outlined in the dying light.

Ever so slowly the sunlight faded from yellow to orange to a deep burning red when suddenly Kevin broke the silence with his booming voice, "The door!" He exploded from across the chamber. I leaped to his side, focused on the vision that appeared etched in the same deep red as the dying sun. There it was, the keyhole, as plain as day. With every eye in the treasure room focused on the door, I swiftly slipped the key into the hole and easily turned it counter-clockwise. With a loud click the glowing outline of an ancient stone door became a carved gap in the solid stone wall. I pushed once and the door swung open as though I had done it every day of my life. Real magic, the kind of which legends are told, was definitely at work in this stately chamber.

With the last of the sunlight we gathered up the torches we had brought along with us into the tunnel. As Charis had anticipated, once the dying sunlight revealed the door we would be left standing next to an open door in the pitch black treasure room. As was usually the case, Charis was right. Because of our training we didn't need to actually see the flint and steel that we used to light the torches. Too bad Danby was not in the tunnel with us to light the torches with a quick burst from his lungs. He waited for us down in the forest, protecting the horses and awaiting our return.

Holding my torch high and leaning through the open doorway, I could make out a long, winding stone stairway falling far away into the darkness. I turned to my friends, looked each in the eye in turn and said, "This is where our paths part. The curse specifically says, 'Descend the stairway all alone.' If I don't return, tell King Edgar I'm sorry that I failed him. Protect the kingdom as the great knights you are . . . give the bards stories to sing with your heroic deeds, and most importantly, take care of my beloved Charis and my best friend, Danby." I hugged Charis and gave her a long kiss, knowing that this might be the last time I ever saw her. I brushed a tear from her cheek, smiled and said, "I love you."

-9-

Raising my torch again, I turned from my companions and began my descent to find the golden ring. There were dusty torches lining the walls in a series of beautifully detailed wall sconces. I lit each in turn as I continued down the winding staircase.

The narrow stairway wound its way steadily downward. I was never in any danger of slipping or falling as these stairs were carved with every bit of the same expertise as the rest of the cave and tunnel complex, as well as the stairs that wound their way up the cliff outside. Along the smooth walls I could see detailed carvings of ancient knights doing battle on horseback. There were knights with swords, spears and bows fighting great beasts that looked mythical and, at the same time, familiar. Many of these same beasts I had seen in the background of my beloved tapestries in the Great Hall at Westerford Castle. The masterful stone carvings were beautiful and, again I wondered who the skilled masons were.

Suddenly, after descending what seemed like a thousand steps, I stepped onto a perfectly level floor. Etched just beneath a fine layer of dust, a jigsaw of seemingly random lines worked their way across the floor at various angles. There seemed to be no distinct pattern to the etchings that spanned the entire floor of the giant room. I held my torch as high as I could but its lightfall barely reached the walls or ceiling. I was in a Great Hall rivaling the dimensions of the Great Hall at Westerford Castle. Torches, just like the ones along the stairway, lined each wall of the Great Hall. As the flame from my torch sparked them to life, the torches blazed brightly and illuminated masterful artwork throughout the hall. Working my way around the room as I lit the torches, I saw how all four walls were decorated with detailed paintings that accented the images etched into the living stone to give a surreal, three-dimensional feel to my surroundings. I realized too, as I made my way around the hall, that each mural depicted the same scenery one would find in the general directions the wall was facing.

The northern wall showed snowy mountains with Mount Uasal as the centerpiece. To the south were the warm seas and sandy beaches we heard about in the songs travelers sang when they came to court, though I had never seen them in person. Lake Machnamh and Dragon Veil Falls were the focus of the western wall, the calm, glassy waters of the lake offset by the roaring falls. The ancient forest of Tranglam spread along the eastern wall. Dark and mysterious, the forest seemed to be an impenetrable tangle of trees and shrubbery. However, there was a clearing in the forest that I had seen before. A ring of giant standing stones carved among the painted forest made them stand out on the mural all the more. Among the stones was a woman in flowing black gowns with her auburn hair billowing as if blown by a strong wind – she appeared to be dancing among the stones. She was the same woman I had seen in the tapestry back at the Great Hall at Westerford Castle!

In the center of the hall, among seven evenly spaced pillars that rose to the ceiling was a stone throne on a pedestal rising two steps from the glass-smooth floor. At first, the throne and dais appeared to be carved out of the floor. On closer inspection I realized that the throne and dais were carved from a single giant boulder that rested in the center of this ancient cave.

My eyes followed the pillars up to the arched ceiling to see that it, too, was detailed with carvings and paintings depicting a three-dimensional image of the night sky. The beauty and grandeur of this incredible room, this living work of art, nearly made me forget why I was there. Nearly, but not quite. My King had been cursed and it was up to me to free him from the curse and restore order to our kingdom.

-10-

The intricately carved throne looked delicate and nearly alive. At the base of the throne were carved roots that appeared to be growing from the base of a great tree trunk and spreading beneath the trunk into the ground in all directions. As my eyes continued to examine the craftsmanship and detail, I realized that, though the throne looked like a growing oak tree, it was actually carved from the giant stone in the center of that great chamber. The seat and arms were carved with detailed wood grain and growth rings just as you would see in the cross-section of any freshly cut tree. Slightly curved, the throne's back was topped with carefully detailed branches complete with leaves and bunches of acorns. A squirrel peering down from behind a branch and a mother bird feeding her babies in an intricately carved nest completed the detail. It was so perfectly done that I felt like I was outside standing before a tree in the forest. Again, I had to shake the distraction from my head. I had to find the ring.

Into the back of the throne was carved the intricate likeness of a dragon. The detail was astonishing and, if I didn't know better, I'd say it was a carved portrait of Danby! Around the curved base of the throne, partly obscured by the carved roots in the ground around the stone tree throne, I could see letters etched into the dais steps:

Whoso wears this golden ring,
Shall be the rightful Dragon King.

Carved into the largest root at the base of the throne was the outline of a small drawer: "Among the roots you'll find a drawer where no one thought to look before," I remembered. The pull on the drawer resembled an acorn that had fallen to the ground to lie among the roots of the mighty Oak. When I gently pulled on the acorn the drawer seemed to be stuck. I pulled again, a bit harder this time but with no more luck than the first.

I leaned forward to look closely at the drawer and noticed what seemed to be a knothole just to the right of the acorn. It was a keyhole. Once more I pulled the golden key and chain from around my neck and guided it into the hole. I turned the key in the hole and, with a metallic click that echoed throughout the cavernous chamber, the drawer was unlocked. I replaced the key around my neck and gently pulled on the acorn. This time the hidden drawer slid out effortlessly, another sign of the master carver's eye for detail.

Within the drawer was a dark blue bag made of velvet. Picking up the bag I knew I had found the ring. To make sure, I opened the bag gently and poured the contents into my open hand. There is was, the ring of kings and the only thing that could release King Edgar from Talia's evil curse. I turned the ring over in my hand and, looking closely, I noticed a tiny engraving on the inside depicting a flying dragon with what appeared to be a crown on his head. Runic symbols were also etched inside the ring. Again, I wished I understood the ancient symbols. I dropped the ring back into the velvet bag and retraced my steps to the stairway. I bolted up them to rejoin my companions.

At the top of the stair I turned for one last look at the miraculous underground hall of the ancient Dragon Kings. In the fading glow of the torchlight, from my vantage point above the hall I could make out the shadowed image of a dragon flying over the kingdom painted or carved into the floor of the hall. Since I had been standing among the lines, I hadn't really seen them until then. The criss-crossing lines on the smooth stone were visible only from my elevated position at the top of the stairway. Dragons had been a part of this kingdom much longer than most people imagined. Based on the carvings and artistry, dragons were not always the terror that recent history would make people believe they were. Dragons, it seemed, were revered in the early history of our kingdom.

With my last glance back at the great underground throne room still fresh in my mind I turned and ran the last few steps to meet my Dragon Knights who still awaited my return armed and ready for anything. I was breathing hard as I burst from the stairwell. The treasure room was the same as when I left it not more than an hour before. But, I had seen amazing things and couldn't wait to share those sights with my companions.

-11-

Those stories of the wonders I had seen would have to wait. My first order was to return as rapidly as possible to King Edgar to place the ring from the stone throne on his finger and return him to his rightful place – King of Westerford. One more thing came suddenly clear to me. As soon as the curse on King Edgar was broken, I knew what my next mission would be. I must find the ring of standing stones in Tranglam Forest. Somehow the woman with auburn hair who dances among the stones was tied to the destiny of the ring, the kingdom, and the history of dragons in Westerford.

Stepping into the treasure room, I knew exactly what we needed to do next and I didn't hesitate. I shouted my orders so there would be no mistake.

"Dragon Knights, arm yourselves for battle and ride to Tranglam Forest as quickly as you can. There is a path into the tangled wood as you approach from the forest road east of Westerford Castle just a mile or two beyond the covered bridge. Do not enter the forest until Danby and I join you. We will be waiting at the crossroads before nightfall tomorrow."

Charis asked the obvious question and immediately answered it herself, "Are you going to take the ring to my uncle? Of course you are. The king is our first priority and has been all along."

"Danby and I will meet you at the crossroads at the edge of the forest before nightfall," I assured them again.

"What do you expect to find in that maze of ancient trees?" asked Garrett.

"Answers," I said shortly. "This adventure has filled me with many questions and the one place in the entire kingdom I've never been is the 'Dorchadas' in Tranglam Forest. I am sure we will find the answers are there," I said with a confidence that I suddenly felt for the first time.

"I don't know what form of danger those answers will take, so we have to be prepared for anything," I continued as I hurried through the tunnel toward Dragon Veil Falls and a final meeting with destiny.

-12-

How Danby got up the cliff stairway and into the chamber behind the falls I didn't pretend to know. But, the drenched floor and pools of water dripping from his muscled back led me to conclude that he had flown through the raging waterfall and landed in the chamber just as his ancestors must have done before him.

I was happy to see him and told him so as I climbed into my position on his back, holding on as tightly as I could trying to avoid getting knocked off as we flew through the wall of water. I never considered the possibility of being swept off his back to be crushed on the rocks at the base of the falls. I knew Danby would never let anything like that happen to me.

In a flash we were off. And, just as fast, I was blinded by the torrent of water that hit me with a cold, rock-hard force like none I'd ever felt.

Danby was so strong and steady that the blast of water didn't faze him. We soared out the other side of Dragon Veil Falls without the slightest dip in our elevation. With a tip of the wings to the right, a tip of the wings to the left and a burst of acceleration, we were dry.

"To King Edgar!" I shouted, and Danby and I were off as if we had been shot from a giant crossbow. Lake Machnamh was a blur beneath Danby's wings. We flew so fast over the lake that I couldn't even see our reflection on the glassy water below.

In no time we were over my childhood village of Sutter but there was no slowing to wave to the children below. Danby was a bolt of lightning in the sky. A quick upturn and we were over the mossy, gray, stone wall, and with a final, great flap of his wings Danby settled into the courtyard of Westerford Castle.

I slid from his shoulders and ran to King Edgar without slowing to nod to guards or servants – they knew my mission and stepped aside when they saw me coming.

-13-

I covered the slate gray floor of the Great Hall in an instant and bound to the king's side in a leap without touching the dais steps. With a pause to nod a bow of respect to King Edgar, I reached into my knapsack for the velvet pouch where my nervous fingers found the ring of gold. With a thought to Talia and ending her horrible curse I placed the ring onto King Edgar's finger, stepped back and watched as a fog seemed to lift from Edgar's eyes. The moment I slipped the ring on the king's finger the glass dagger instantly melted as if it were made of ice. His eyes fluttered, then opened, and King Edgar smiled weakly at me.

As one, the crowd that had followed me into the Great Hall let out a collective sigh then burst into cheering and deafening applause at the sight of the king's awakening. He was finally free from that terrible place between life and death.

With a weak wave of his hand Edgar bid me come closer, he had something for my ears alone. As I moved in, he began to whisper in my ear, his voice barely audible even as close as I was. The king said, "Find Talia, Nat. Do her no harm; she is not my enemy. This is not over yet. There is much to be done before this spell is finally broken."

Clearly not understanding, I tried to speak but the King silenced me with another wave and said, "You will find her in Tranglam Forest. In the dell you will find a circle of ancient standing stones. Talia will be there when the moon is full. Listen for her song and heed the words. I must join you there. The spell is not yet broken." His voice trailed away as he gave me a smile of gratitude.

-14-

Knowing the Dragon Knights would meet me at the crossroads near Tranglam Forest the next day I took a bit of time to tend to Danby. I made sure he had fresh food and water and clean hay in his "lair" for a comfortable night's sleep. Once Danby was down for the night I made a bit of time for myself. I washed up and indulged myself with a hot meal for the first time in days. A pang of guilt crept in with my meal, knowing that my team of Dragon Knights, including my darling Charis, was somewhere out on the trail eating a cold dinner and sleeping under the stars. I knew they would not begrudge me a hot meal and a sound night's sleep.

My meal was delicious, however, my night's sleep was anything but sound. Each time I settled into a deep sleep I saw Talia among the ancient standing stones in Tranglam Forest. Her dirty gray hair and ink-black cloak flowing in the faint breeze, her black, lifeless eyes piercing me while, without moving her lips, her song called me to her. A singsong voice echoed in my ears as I awoke with a start hearing the same song over and over again:

Stir the cauldron, watch it roil,
Fan the flames that make it boil.
Tail of lizard, wing of bat,
Egg of pigeon, bacon fat,
Leaves of ivy, bones of hen,
Hide us from the sight of men.
A ring of stones stands strong and tall
And guards us like a castle wall.
In forest dark where evils lurk,

Spells and potions do their work.
Out of sight our magic lies,
Hidden from all prying eyes.
We dance here within Tranglam Dell
Until one comes to break the spell.
Hid by standing stones around,
We'll be set free when we are found.
When seven knights, both young and bold,
Match symbols seven from days of old,
When Dragon Fire surrounds the Dell,
Cool rain will wash away the spell.
Forbidden love will bloom anon,
Sadness will, at last, be gone.
Then joins a pair from days gone past,
To reunite true love at last.

-15-

At dawn I arose, dressed and hurried to awaken Danby. That night, under a full moon, was the night my Dragon Knights and I would find Talia in the forest among the standing stones. King Edgar would join us in the clearing to break the spell at last, and put king and kingdom to rights once and for all.

As I rushed down the gray stone hallway toward Danby's "lair", Ollamh appeared, as if by magic, from the dark shadows of a doorway and bade me follow him. I hesitated for a moment but, knowing Ollamh would never sidetrack my mission if he didn't have something valuable to add, I slipped into the darkened doorway and followed my tutor. A winding stone staircase led down into the underbelly of the castle. Black moss seemed to ooze from cracks between the ancient stones and the sound of water dripping in places unseen kept rhythm with our quickly descending footsteps. Ollamh carried his walking stick aloft and from its end a dim glow gave off just enough light so that I could safely follow him down the staircase to the damp chamber beneath the castle. I'd never seen him use his walking stick that way before. There was far more about this man than I ever imagined.

This room, it turns out, doubled as Ollamh's study and living quarters. A layer of dust blanketed the aged and tattered leather bound books and dog-eared parchment rolls scattered about with ancient writing scribbled across the yellowed pages. The room was a mess, but it seemed Ollamh knew exactly where to find what he was looking for.

Crooked old fingers walked the length of a cluttered shelf high up a wooden bookcase that was built into a niche in the wall. He stood on tip-toe with his head tipped up shaking back and forth as he passed over volume after volume finally withdrawing a small brown leather book with gold lettering on its spine. Ollamh whispered, "Ah, ha! This is the piece I want to share with you, Nat."

Losing patience that I had delayed my quest for an old book, I asked, "Ollamh, what could this old book have to do with saving King Edgar from that old hag's curse?" In his usual steady voice, with a wry smile and a gleam in his eye, Ollamh said, "Everything."

He settled himself into a large wooden chair and nodded toward another so that I would do the same. Although I felt a sense of urgency, I obliged, knowing that to refuse would only prolong this delay.

-16-

Licking his fingers, Ollamh leafed through the old book until he came across a page with a turned-down corner. "Here we are," Ollamh's old voice creaked, then, clearing his throat he began to read.

"In the golden age of Westerford, King Edmund ruled with a firm but noble hand. His subjects honored him and the kingdom was safe and happy. Edmund was a good king, but a shadow loomed darkly over the kingdom in the form of Laghairt, the dragon. While the people of the kingdom lived in relative prosperity, there could be no true peace with constant fear hanging over them. One evening, while brooding in his Great Hall, King Edmund vowed to end the threat once and for all."

At this point in Ollamh's reading I cut him off, "I know all about King Edmund killing Laghairt, everyone in Westerford knows that story!" I said with an annoyed panic that Ollamh was wasting precious time in my efforts to save the king. "Please, get to the point. I've found the golden ring but Edgar is still hanging somewhere between this world and the next – I must do something to help him!" I shouted.

With a calm that only he could demonstrate at a time like this, Ollamh nodded and flipped through a few more pages. Then, just as slowly as before, continued reading. "The dragon, Laghairt, was dead. King Edmund held his severed head aloft for all to see. But, as the bells began to ring happily in the church steeples and the people of the kingdom rejoiced as one, King Edmund collapsed in a heap from the injuries he received during his terrible battle with the beast, Laghairt."

"As Edmund lay in his chambers, propped up with several pillows and attended by the finest surgeons in the kingdom, he called his two sons to his side: Edgar and Egbert, or 'Bert', who was two years younger than his older brother." At that I interrupted again. "Ollamh, that isn't right. Bert was the eldest. Bert took over upon Edmund's death. What's going on here?" I asked, completely confused.

"May I continue?" Asked Ollamh. I sat back in my chair and nodded beginning to understand that there was something more to this story that few people knew. "He called his two sons to his side: Edgar and Egbert, who was two years younger than his older brother. In a pained whisper, Edmund spoke to the young men. He spoke of the kingdom and the need to take great care to ensure that the people were happy and had everything they needed to live long, fruitful lives. It was the king's responsibility to protect his people so that they could raise their families as important members of society – the people are important. King Edmund also spoke of his love for his sons and his pride in the young men they had become. He told them that he knew they would both make great kings in their own way and that they must marry soon so that the royal line could continue. Remember, King Edmund continued with increasing difficulty, the only requirement in choosing a bride is that the young lady must be a born citizen of Westerford. This law has been passed down for generations and must never be broken. You both will be great kings, Edmund whispered, and I love you both. With those words, Edmund closed his eyes and peacefully slipped away from this world to begin his journey in the next."

Ollamh paused and closed his eyes for a moment. I thought he was finished, but I waited to see what would come next. I finally understood that Ollamh was leading me to something that would help me save King Edgar.

-17-

When Ollamh opened his eyes there was a gleam in them as if he were ready to cry, but his lips curled into a smile and he whispered, "I loved King Edmund. He was a great and noble king. I tutored Edmund just as I have tutored you, Nat."

Without another word Ollamh reopened the old book and flipped a few more pages. Regaining his focus he again began to read, "While riding through Tranglam Forest one day, Prince Edgar stumbled upon an ancient ring of standing stones. Inside the ring was a beautiful maiden with flowing red hair and piercing green eyes. Edgar introduced himself and learned that her name was Rachel.

Every day, from that day forward, Edgar would ride the five miles from the castle into Tranglam Forest to visit Rachel. They spent many hours walking through the woods talking about everything. They enjoyed being together, holding hands, and sharing noontime meals. On warm summer days they would swim in the forest streams and then lie on flat boulders in the sun to dry. Those were magical days for Edgar and Rachel. They fell in love and decided it was time to make their love public.

In all their days together, through countless hours of deep conversation, Edgar had failed to mention one small detail about himself. In a few short months Edgar would be crowned King of Westerford in a ceremony before the entire Kingdom. Although there was still great sadness at the heroic passing of King Edmund, the future of the Kingdom was bright and Prince Edgar was beloved by the people. Edgar had found his queen, the love of his life, and Rachel would become his wife, Queen of Westerford.

"One sunny afternoon while lying side by side in a meadow watching the clouds drift by in the blue sky, Edgar turned to Rachel and said, 'There's something that I need to tell you before we get married, Rachel." With a troubled expression and a slight tremble in her voice, Rachel replied, 'No matter what it is, Edgar, it will never change the way I feel about you – my love for you runs deep and strong and nothing will ever change that feeling – ever.'"

"Edgar smiled softly and looked deeply into Rachel's bright green eyes. With a slight laugh he said, 'You act as if what I have to tell you is bad news. My love, I, too, have sworn my love to you and nothing will ever change the way I feel about you. What I have to tell you is a wonderful thing and will only make our life together more magical, if that is even possible,' Edgar said with an honesty and love that welled up from deep within him. 'Rachel,' he said with an edge of excitement in his voice, 'In four months' time, on the first full moon of the new year, I am to be crowned King of Westerford – I want to marry you and I want you to be my Queen, forever.'

"Rachel smiled shyly at first. Her bright eyes filled with tears that spilled down her cheeks. Her hands flew to her face and she began to shake with sobs of sadness that Edgar had never seen before. He reached for her and hugged her closely wondering with all his heart what he had said to upset Rachel so deeply. There were no words to say, so the two stood in that meadow, in the forest, on that glorious summer day, embraced in a hug borne of deep love and deeper sorrow because it would be their last.

"Slowly, Rachel's sobbing subsided and she pulled away from Edgar. With a quivering voice she said, 'Oh, Edgar, future King of Westerford, I cannot marry you. I love you with all my heart and soul and know that I will never love another the way that I love you. But, the fact is that I was not born in Westerford and it is well known that the king can only marry a naturally born citizen of the kingdom.' With that Rachel burst into tears again and, with a final look into Edgar's eyes, turned and walked back into the forest toward her home deep in the woods.

"Edgar just watched her walk away without a word until she disappeared into the shadows. He mounted his great white horse and turned slowly back to the castle. On his way back to Westerford Castle, Edgar decided that he would relinquish his throne, allowing Bert to become king in his place. Edgar would search Tranglam Forest until he found Rachel again. He loved her and would marry her if it was the last thing he ever did."

-18-

Ollamh paused and turned toward a dusty mirror that hung crookedly on the stone wall of his underground chamber. He held his staff up high and mumbled a few words that I couldn't understand as he swayed back and forth in front of the glass. He seemed to be in some sort of trance. Magically a picture appeared in the distance and Ollamh gazed at it as if looking out a window in the gray stone wall. In the distance he could see Tranglam Forest, a blue-gray mist hung around the treetops, and the orange sun sat low in the late morning sky. Menacing storm clouds appeared to be closing in around the forest. He turned to me then with what looked like a tear in his eye and began to explain, "You see, Nat, Edgar is the True King of Westerford. He gave up his claim to the throne to marry Rachel, his one true love. His world came crashing down when he returned to the forest searching for her. Every day Edgar looked for her, calling her name, but he could never find her. Travelers would tell stories of a beautiful woman dancing in the forest among seven ancient standing stones. But, when Edgar arrived, there was no one there," Ollamh explained with pain in his voice that trailed off into a thoughtful silence. "Rachel's mother, Talia, angered by the hurt she saw in her daughter's eyes, bewitched the forest and cast a spell that would keep Rachel and Edgar apart forever," Ollamh sighed almost speaking to himself.

"Where did Rachel go?" I asked softly as if breaking a spell. Ollamh jumped a little, like he had forgotten I was in the room with him, and said, "Oh, she was there, in the forest, dancing among the stones just as the travelers said she was. She is there right now and will remain there forever, unless . . ." With that

Ollamh's voice trailed off again, and, again, he seemed lost in thought.

"Unless," he finally continued, "Talia's spell is broken once and for all!" Ollamh nearly shouted this last part.

"That's what I've come to do," I said, wondering what Ollamh thought I was doing all this time.

"I've found the key," I said, "I've located the door to the ancient throne room, and I've recovered the True King's golden ring!"

Ollamh looked me directly in both eyes, took my face in his crooked old hands and pulled me close. His grizzled old face shattered in a broad smile and he nearly shouted, "Not that spell, my boy!"

-19-

Tearing through the old book, Ollamh quickly found the page he sought and read the final piece of the puzzle:

Among the ancient standing stones
A maiden dances all alone.
A king drifts between life and death
Saved only by a dragon's breath.
Seven knights and seven stones
Bear witness to a magic throne.
True love is the real key
The ring is but a token,
Among the stones they reunite
The spell, then, will be broken.

Ollamh closed the book, tossed it on the table amid the clutter of books, scrolls and dust, and turned me toward the door.

"We must hurry," he shouted as we nearly ran down the gray corridor, up the winding stone stairway and into the courtyard where Danby waited, ready to fly.

Danby gave me a nod as I leapt onto his back. Imagine my surprise as Ollamh scrambled onto Danby's back right behind me as if we'd done that every day. Danby responded with an easy nod, fully understanding that something important must be happening. One thrust of his mighty wings and we were airborne and on our way over the high castle walls.

"To the crossroads of Tranglam Forest!" I shouted and felt Ollamh grab me a bit tighter as Danby banked hard to the east. I could see the forest on the horizon but that was the extent of my knowledge. I, honestly, wasn't sure what to expect as we soared into the unknown.

-20-

Gray clouds seemed to press hard down upon the forest making our flight to the crossroads dark and ominous. I could feel trouble brewing but I wasn't sure where it would come from. I had to be ready for anything. My Dragon Knights should be waiting for me at the crossroads as planned, I thought to myself as Danby skillfully glided just above the treetops careful to stay out of the ever-darkening clouds. Flying in a storm of that magnitude was more dangerous than one might imagine. We had learned the hard way how disorienting thick clouds can be – not to mention the blinding flashes of lightning and deafening thunder, flying in that kind of weather spelled disaster. Danby knew the danger as well as I and chose to stay clear of the storm, deftly maneuvering low among the treetops instead.

Approaching the crossroads I couldn't see my friends. My heart sank for an instant to think that they weren't there to help finish our quest. Suddenly, as Danby banked low toward the crossroads, nearly dumping Ollamh and causing him to squeeze me a little tighter than I would have liked, I noticed movement in a clearing on a green hilltop just west of the crossroads. It was the Dragon Knights and they were in trouble.

Back to back they crouched in a tight circle atop the hill with their weapons drawn. Danby saw them too and needed no encouragement from me to increase his speed. He leaned hard to the left as I drew my sword ready to join my comrades against a foe that I could not yet see. Angling low and fast, the trees blurred in the corners of my eyes, as my entire focus was on my knights and what danger they were in at that moment. With a great flap of his wings, Danby landed on top of the hill right in the middle of my circle of friends. I slid quickly from his back and, just as quickly, Danby was airborne again with my aged teacher, Ollamh, still clinging desperately to his neck.

With sword drawn I took my place in the circle of Dragon Knights atop that green hill. With a laugh, Ryan shouted as he notched an arrow on his bow and let fly into the surrounding forest, "It's about time you joined the fun, Nat, a few more minutes and you would have missed it completely!" I followed the path of his arrow with my eyes as it buried itself to the fletching in the chest of a great, snarling, wolf. With a final howl of pain, the massive wolf fell over where it stood among the lifeless bodies of dozens more of the foul creatures. It was obvious, at a glance, that this battle between my knights and these wolves had been raging for quite some time. The Dragon Knights had fought well, for wolves were piled everywhere and only three remained to circle the hilltop, their thick fur matted with foaming sweat, slobber dripping from their giant fangs and death reflected in their yellow eyes.

In an instant, the largest of the wolves lunged directly at me. I stepped quickly to my left avoiding his sudden attack. With my sword already drawn I slashed after the wolf with a back-hand swipe that cut the wolf from his hind leg to his ribs on the side of his body, leaving a gaping wound from which there would be no recovery. Rolling to its side, the wolf righted itself and made a final leap toward me. I was ready for him this time and drove my sword deep into his chest. As the glow faded from the wolf's yellow eyes, his two surviving companions fled into the darkness of Tranglam Forest leaving their many dead and wounded comrades behind.

While I caught my breath from my brief struggle with the enormous wolf, I looked around at the rest of my Dragon Knights. Bloody and exhausted, my friends began to laugh aloud as they realized that they were all alive and unharmed. I ran to Charis and hugged her tightly as I smiled at the rest of my knights over her shoulder. As Charis reluctantly pulled away from my embrace, I asked Garrett what had happened.

"We chose this hilltop to make our camp last night so that we could keep watch on the surrounding forest," he began to explain. "Almost from the moment you left us at Dragon Veil Falls we had a strange sensation that we were being watched or even followed. It is not a very long ride from the falls to the crossroads. It should not have taken us more than half a day to make it. But, our horses were skittish, frightened even. Every step, it seemed, drew us deeper into a forbidding darkness, and our horses needed coaxing the whole way," Garrett explained in a voice that sounded at once exhausted and alarmed.

Chase spoke up concerned, "Just look around, Nat. Our horses were right – they knew that very real danger lurked right around the corner!"

I looked around then to see our seven beautiful horses badly wounded by the wolves. Some staggered and some stood still, but all bore savage wounds from the battle. It would be a miracle if the horses survived the ordeal.

-21-

I needed time to think. But, there really wasn't time to waste. I walked slowly to the edge of the clearing to gather my thoughts. Staring into the vastness of Tranglam Forest I focused, not on the tangle of ancient trees, but a single branch, hanging low, on a single tree. Among the mottled sticks of that single branch I watched a hairy, brown spider spinning an intricate web. A trap set for an unsuspecting insect that might wander aimlessly into that tiny corner of the sprawling forest.

In that instant everything became crystal clear. Talia had set a trap in the forest just like this tiny spider web. I would not become that unsuspecting insect. I would not wander aimlessly into Talia's web. More importantly, I would not lead my Dragon Knights into a deadly trap in the ancient forest of Tranglam.

Hurrying straight down the forest road was exactly what Talia would expect us to do – we were young and we were in a rush. Instead, we would need to reach the circle of standing stones by some other way. But, how?

I quickly returned to the center of the clearing where my Dragon Knights were recovering from their ferocious battle with the wolves. When I rejoined them, my team rose, as one, from where they were resting, ready for whatever came next.

Danby and Ollamh had returned. I saw that Ollamh was tending to the injured horses. Talking to them soothingly, he spread some sort of natural ointment into the horse's wounds that he had made by mixing mud, roots, and crushed plants. As I approached, Ollamh was wrapping each animal's injuries with cloth strips that he had torn from his own tunic.

-22-

"Ollamh," I said with urgency in my voice, "think back. Is there another way into Tranglam Forest besides the old forest road? Talia will be expecting us to use the main road and we need to arrive unannounced."

With his usual thoughtful expression, Ollamh paused, his eyes glazed over as he considered my question. Finally, he said, "There is another path, a darker path, that passes into the part of Tranglam that the locals call the 'Dorchadas.' That track will lead you to the standing stones. About a half mile into the woods on the forest road a little-used route turns off toward the heart of Tranglam. I will stay with Danby and we will meet you when you arrive at your destination. You will know the path when you see a wishing well. Do not drink from the well no matter how thirsty you are!" Ollamh warned, "The water is cursed and will cause you to see things that may or may not actually be there. Follow the trail and do not stray. Many travelers have said that they heard beautiful voices singing to them off in the woods. And, many travelers never returned."

I pulled Ollamh aside and whispered, "Return with Danby to Westerford Castle. Dress King Edgar for the chill night air and meet us at the ancient stone circle in the 'Dorchadas' before the full moon reaches its peak in the night sky." Ollamh began to protest. Then, with a knowing smile, seemed to understand. Without another word Ollamh climbed onto Danby's back and in a twinkle they were airborne and flying west toward the castle and King Edgar.

I could see Tranglam Forest from where I stood on that green hilltop and I knew that we were less than a mile from the crossroads. According to Ollamh it was about a half mile into the woods beyond the crossroads where the path turned off towards the "Dorchadas" in the heart of Tranglam. Wasting no time, we gathered our weapons and began our march into the darkest depths of the forest leaving our horses tethered to the low-hanging branches of an ancient oak.

-23-

The rising full moon lighted our way with a silvery glow. We stayed close together, with weapons drawn, prepared for anything. Our imaginations ran wild with anticipation. The darkness of the surrounding forest seemed to press in on us from all sides. But, we heeded Ollamh's warning and carefully stuck to the path no matter what.

Suddenly, as if from beyond a great barrier, I heard the sweetest voice singing or chanting a rhythmic tune that seemed to draw me toward a clearing just ahead. Standing in the forest shadows the moonlight revealed a great circle of stones in the center of the clearing. There were seven stones carved of gray rock that seemed unnatural in this part of the kingdom. Each stone stood taller than a man and increased in width from bottom to top. I wondered how deep into the ground those narrow bases must be buried. And, I wondered if they had been built there by the same expert masons who created the magnificent stairs and caverns of Dragon Veil Falls. The voice was coming from within the circle and seemed to grow louder as we approached but I could see no one within the ancient ring.

A thin blanket of fog shrouded the floor among the standing stones as we neared the sacred ground. Without seeing her I could imagine Talia dancing within the stone ring, her hypnotic song echoing from the ring of stones into the surrounding forest to die away among the gray and green undergrowth. Step by agonizing step we inched closer to the stones. I had given the order to spread out and we advanced from behind each stone – there were seven stones and we were seven knights who had come to witness a meeting between the Lady of Tranglam Forest and King Edgar of Westerford.

-24-

As I drew closer there appeared to be a small pile of stones within the circle. But, as I stared, a moonbeam broke through the trees and I could see that the stones were not just randomly piled. They had been stacked so that they created a large seat. This was no ordinary chair. It was fashioned to resemble a large throne built for royalty. The stones were seamlessly fitted without mortar and the craftsmanship was impeccable. Staring at the throne I could see that it faced Westerford Castle, which was situated upon its stately hill, the high gray walls reaching toward the heavens, firelight glowing invitingly from every window.

No one was visible within the standing stone circle, but I could hear that bewitching voice singing or chanting over and over what, at first, seemed to be a song. As I continued to listen, the words seemed mournful, sorrowful. It was clear that, whoever was singing, was under some kind of enchantment.

Eerie and beautiful at the same time, I began to wonder whose voice it was that was singing the same song from my dream and how I could help release the sad singer from her spell. She sang:

Stir the cauldron, watch it roil,
Fan the flames that make it boil.
Tail of lizard, wing of bat,
Egg of pigeon, bacon fat,
Leaves of ivy, bones of hen,
Hide us from the sight of men.
A ring of stones stands strong and tall
And guards us like a castle wall.

In forest dark where evils lurk,
Spells and potions do their work.
Out of sight our magic lies,
Hidden from all prying eyes.
We dance here within Tranglam Dell
Until one comes to break the spell.
Hid by standing stones around,
We'll be set free when we are found.
When seven knights, both young and bold,
Match symbols seven from days of old,
When Dragon Fire surrounds the Dell,
Cool rain will wash away the spell.
Forbidden love will bloom anon,
Sadness will, at last, be gone.
Then joins a pair from days gone past,
To reunite true love at last.

As we entered the clearing just outside the great stone circle, we were all constantly scanning the area for any sign of danger. The stones were much taller than I had pictured. Giants must have carved them many years before. No one was here, although I could hear the faint rhythmic singsong chanting the words from my dream. Was I still dreaming or was this magical scene real?

Looking at the ancient stones I noticed that each, though roughly carved, had a smooth circle near the top with a runic symbol etched deep into the stone at the center of the smooth circle. Each stone bore a different rune. Suddenly I understood, I recognized those ancient symbols. The runes matched the marks on the Dragon Knights' armor – "Seven knights match seven stones!" I shouted causing the rest of the knights to jump in fright.

"Find the stone with a rune that matches your own, quickly," My anxious voice echoed in the quiet forest. We drew our weapons and aligned ourselves before the stones that matched our signs. At the exact moment we stopped moving and stood silently in front of our stones a great flash of lightning struck the pile of stones in the center of the circle blinding us momentarily and creating a great cloud of white smoke within the ring.

The brilliant flash and cloud of smoke made me realize that the full moon had broken through a hole in the clouds and Tranglam Forest was awash in a mysterious glow. Rising high above the clearing the dazzling full moon shed its silvery light among the standing stones. But, the darkness of the surrounding forest and ring of black clouds was stifling. At that moment I recalled the rhythmic words from my dream:

When Dragon Fire surrounds the Dell,
Cool rain will wash away the spell.

-25-

At that moment I saw a shadow pass over the clearing. I knew who it was and smiled at the timing. I called to Danby. When my friend landed the Dragon Knights helped Ollamh from his back. I looked at Ollamh wondering where King Edgar was. He gave me a nod and a smile assuring me that the king was safely nearby.

I moved in close to whisper into Danby's ear. A great flap of his wings let me know he understood. He soared with ease, circling the ancient stone ring. Suddenly, a powerful stream of fire burst from Danby's lungs lighting the ancient brittle trees at the edge of the clearing. Encircled by burning forest, we stepped as one crowding the center of the circle. The brilliant fire gave all the light we needed to see what would happen next.

Without warning the ominous clouds that surrounded the clearing released a downpour that put out the fire almost as quickly as it had started. In a matter of minutes the great wall of smoke and steam created by the fire lifted.

As if by magic, in place of the gnarled oaks of Tranglam stood a grove of tall, young aspen trees. The white bark of the thin trunks and the shimmering golden leaves revealed the promise of rebirth in the forest.

As the smoke cleared away and my vision returned to me, I could see Rachel, the beautiful woman with auburn hair. The same woman I'd seen on the tapestry in the Great Hall back at Westerford Castle.

The throne-shaped pile of rocks in the center of the circle was gone. In its place was a magnificent throne carved out of stone and made to resemble the trunk of an ancient oak tree.

I realized it was an exact replica of the throne from the Great Hall beneath Dragon Veil Falls.

Suddenly, from behind the throne stepped Talia. My knights moved toward her, weapons drawn. In spite of the king's warning not to harm her, I wanted with all my heart to finish that witch with my own sword, I held up my hand and the Dragon Knights instantly stopped. No one took an eye off of Talia, but no one made another move toward her.

Still dressed in her ink-black cloak and carrying her ancient walking stick she had somehow transformed. At last I saw the difference, Talia was smiling and her eyes were no longer angry, black and lifeless. Just like Rachel's, Talia's eyes were a radiant green that seemed to smile. She looked genuinely happy; nothing like the evil hag I had met that night at Westerford Castle. I no longer feared Talia, the dragon fire and subsequent rain had truly washed away the spell.

-26-

In an instant, a flash, everything became clear to me. Ollamh stepped into the clearing and, taking the maiden by the hand he knelt and said, "Rachel, the spell that has bound you for so many years has been broken. Your one true love, King Edgar, is on his way at this moment to claim you as his bride, if you will have him."

The Dragon Knights looked bewildered and wondered what Ollamh was talking about. Of course I had heard the tale already. Rather than explain, I decided to let this scene play out in its own way. I turned to send Danby to get King Edgar, but Ollamh was, as always, one step ahead of me. He was truly wise.

Within seconds, a great breeze began to disrupt the leaves of the young aspen forest around us. The trees swayed and the branches creaked as though they would break. A final gust and Danby landed softly in the center of the ancient stone circle with King Edgar, still clinging weakly to his muscled back. A smile creased the king's face as we helped him down and seated him gently on the stone throne surrounded by the Dragon Knights and the great stone circle. He sat up tall and strong on the throne. Edgar seemed to be recovering his strength before us. The king's smile broadened when his eyes met Rachel's. She returned his smile with a shy one of her own.

Rachel stepped toward the king and, as their eyes met, the years and the heartache seemed to melt away. Edgar stood up to his full height and stepped to Rachel taking her in his arms before he spoke.

"Many years ago," began Edgar, "When I discovered that I could not marry you, and be King of Westerford, I surrendered my throne to my younger brother, Bert." A gasp of understanding ran through the gathered Dragon Knights as Edgar continued, "I spent many years searching for you here in the forest, but because of this curse I could never find you again. I know that as long as I am King of Westerford I will never be able to marry you, Rachel. Therefore," King Edgar said turning to face me but still talking to Rachel, "I am prepared, once again, to relinquish my throne to my heir, Sir Nathaniel, the True Dragon King."

A great lump caught in my throat as I searched for some response. All I could do was drop to a knee before the king, who reached up, gently removed his golden crown, and placed it even more gently on my bowed head. In his deep and powerful voice Edgar said, "Rise King Nathaniel of Westerford and grant me permission, if you will, to marry my love, Rachel, the Lady of Tranglam Forest."

-27-

At last I understood what the curse really meant.

"True love is the real key, the ring is but a token, among the stones they reunite, the spell, then, will be broken."

It was my turn to smile broadly as I rose nervously to my feet, the golden crown snug on my head, and said, "Edgar, I will grant your request and take on the great responsibility as King of Westerford under one condition."

At that Edgar's brow rose wondering what possible request I would make of him.

"Edgar, I grant you permission to marry the Lady Rachel if you will swear your allegiance to me as adviser to the king for as long as you shall live."

Edgar hugged me tightly then, remembering himself, knelt before me saying, "I humbly accept your condition and swear my loyalty to you and the Kingdom of Westerford for as long as I live." Edgar drew his great sword, Cumhacht, and handed it to me jewel-encrusted pommel first. He held onto the point of the sword and gently kissed the end as a sign of his loyalty. Edgar removed the golden ring that I had recovered from the cave beneath Dragon Veil Falls, slipped it onto my right ring finger, and said, "You, King Nathaniel, are the True Dragon King."

"Rise Edgar and claim your bride," I said finally, stepping back among my Dragon Knights and taking my rightful place beside Charis.

Edgar stepped to Rachel, taking her by both hands and looking at his reflection in her green eyes. With an understanding smile, Edgar got down on one knee and said, "Rachel, the moon is full and I am no longer King of Westerford. As I said so long ago, I have sworn my love to you and nothing will ever change the way I feel about you. I want to marry you and I want you to be my wife, forever."

A single tear rolled down Rachel's cheek as she looked back into Edgar's eyes and said, "I would like to ask my mother for her blessing in this marriage." With that Rachel turned to Talia and said, "Mother, these brave and noble knights have solved your riddle, your curse for my lost love is lifted and, after all these years, my one true love stands before me. Will you give us your blessing?"

With a broad smile on her weathered face Talia replied, "Your happiness is all I've ever wanted, Rachel. Everything I have done I have done for you, my only child. I had to discover whether Edgar still truly loved you. He has proven that he is true and honorable, and has demonstrated his undying love for you. I humbly give my blessing to you both and ask that you both find it within your hearts to forgive me." Edgar and Rachel bowed their heads in thanks and forgiveness to Talia and turned to face Ollamh.

From within the folds of his robe Ollamh withdrew a small, leather bound book. His crooked old fingers fumbled through the volume until he found the page from which he intended to read. What began as a rescue became a wedding.

The spell broken, Edgar and Rachel were married that night. Ollamh performed the ceremony and there, bathed in the silver glow of the full moon, surrounded by a magical grove of aspens in the center of Tranglam Forest, their wedding was witnessed by six Dragon Knights, a Dragon named Danby, and me, the True Dragon King of Westerford.

GLOSSARY OF UNFAMILIAR NAMES

Achrann —	"Confrontation"
Brainse —	"Branch"
Comharsa —	"Neighbor"
Cumhacht —	"Power"
Dorchadas —	"Darkness"
Duille —	"Leaf"
Laghairt —	"Lizard"
Machnamh —	"Reflection"
Ollamh —	"Professor"
Tranglam —	"Confusion"
Uasal —	"Noble"

SPECIAL THANKS FOR YOUR SUPPORT

Albert Rodriguez
Craig Womack
Deby Daniel
Liz and Andy Calbreath
Susan Prince
Donna M. Horn
Carly Dreme Calbreath
Nancy and Shana Androus
Sam Trad
Margie Flores
Frankie Fikrle
Liz Steblay
Greg Womack
Wendy Best
Jill Harris
Debi Glaser
Yasuyuki and Judy Owada
Mike Bagg
Linda
Anne Perry Franken
Karen Chastain
Maria Magana-Saenz
Jori Woodbury
Mark and Kathleen Fish
Kay Womack
Sherry Smith
Maeda Family
Garrett Womack
Darren Paxton
Kevin Haggerty
John DeVries
Bill and Carol Grant
Rissa
Don Haskins
Mary Mooney
S.R. Weaver
Kyle Mahan
Genung Family
Debra Lelong
Carrie Mahan
Shad Kirkland
Michael Fish
Doug Marques
Morgana Wyman
Diane Michaelis
Nanette Vazquez
Jon Aed
Christine Rettig

Karen Rodriguez
Jessica Gustafsson
Toni Preciado
Eileen Sanborn
Sue Yeoman
Jeanne Jackson Raynes
Marie Hada
Justin Price
Jacob Yarmuth
Rick Gordon
Elizabeth Grimes
Jody Wolfe
Carlyle Poole
Michelle Moore
Sarah Simko
Romeo Espinal
Julie and Stan Waite
Heather Seaton
Patrick Smith
Christopher Woychak
Ruth Wardschenk
Angie Buck (Rivas)
Larry Hills
Linda DeBaun
Terry Marino
Scott Kennedy
Zach Requejo
Clifford "Chibby" Chapman
Zachary Heath
Raleigh Littles
Christina Lee Riley Chartier

BIO

Darryl Womack's love for story-telling was spurred from family camping trips and his many colorful tales shared around the campfire in the backwoods of California. A high school English teacher by day, Womack is now bringing those vivid campfire fables to life in his new book, Tales of Westerford. When he is not writing, Womack enjoys the outdoors, traveling, mountain biking, reading, and spending time with family and friends. A graduate of Humboldt State University, he currently resides in Redlands, California with his wife of 27 years, Patty. Together they have three sons, Garrett, Kevin, and Christopher.

ACKNOWLEDGMENTS:

Being new to this publishing game I had no idea how many people were involved in a project like this. I'm sure that a brief mention here cannot begin to repay my immense gratitude to you all for the kind words, support, and positive feedback you gave for my tale.

Thanks to my wonderful wife, Patty. My best friend. Not sure what I did to deserve you in my life. Words can't express my feelings.

Thanks to my boys: Garrett; Kevin; and Chris. You guys are an inspiration to me every day in more ways than you will ever know. So many years ago you asked me to tell you a story.

Thanks to my amazing family: dad; mom; brother; sister; in-laws; nieces; nephews; and cousins for encouraging me along with positive comments and support – my whole life, including throughout this process.

Thanks to the kids that read it and gave feedback on what you liked and what you didn't. Nicole, Mitchell, Emma, and Max.

Thanks to my friends and colleagues at Yucaipa High School for reading my rough drafts and encouraging me to push forward with this thing. Stacy, Melinda, Teri, Nanette, Jessica, Melissa, and Amanda.

Thanks to Anna McHargue, my editor, for taking the time to read an old friend's story "just to give advice." Just look what you've done!

Thanks to Mark Russell and the rest of the crew at Elevate for taking a chance on my little story.